CONTENTS

Summary	4
Introduction	5
Dinner Date	7
The Morning After the Dinner Date	13
One Room Over	17
Through the Wall	24
Enter Caleb	28
Daytime Reports	30
Let's Do A Deal	34
Warm and Moist	38
What To Do?	42
Part One: Some Facts of It	46
Rationale	47
Setting Parameters	51
Caleb's Wrath	54
Feeding Caleb's Ego	58
Making the Rounds	61

The Least Favorite	65
Part Two: Is it Starting to Make Sense?	69
Job Stuff	75
Cheers	79
Answers for Consumptions	81
Morning Lights?	86
MD+ 1 minus 1	90
Hearing and Seeing are Senses	94
Buh Bye Kayla	96
Not a Savior	98
Part Three: A New Household	100
New Co-Workers	101
Howdy	104
Regular Tour	107
The GRAND Tour	111
Flatness	119
Dex's Real Room	123
Torrid Vital	126
Part Four: Keeping Cool	130
New and Better	131
And Freddy Watched	135
Cleaning House	139
Hosed	144
Household Meeting	148

A note from the dark mind of Sea Caummisar　152

SEA CAUMMISAR

Ethically Questionable #1 Extreme Horror

From the dark mind of Sea Caummisar

SEA CAUMMISAR

Copyright © 2025 by Sea Caummisar

All rights reserved. No portion of this book may be reproduced in any form without permission from the publisher, except as permitted by U.S. copyright law. For permissions contact sharoncheatham81@gmail.com

This is entirely a work of fiction, pulled out of my own imagination. All characters and events are not real (fictitious). If there are any similarities to real persons, living or dead, it is purely coincidental.

I write stories about fake people. Fictional. Not real.
Some of them are not nice and they do bad things.
Be kind to one another.
A place like this one PROBABLY does not exist.
Or maybe a place like this does exist, but this story is not based upon a specific place.

SUMMARY

Kayla and Freddy met online, and she thought he might be the man of her dreams. Charming, attractive, attentive, and considerate.

Until he invites her over for a dinner, prepared by him.

There's something in the food, and she doesn't like it one bit.

Unbeknownst to Kayla, Freddy has a stressful job and now she's a part of it, against her will.

Warning: violent scenes of torture

INTRODUCTION

There is hair growing from the roof of my mouth. The thick coat of cilia aggravates my tongue, robbing me of my speech; slurring and curving every single one of my spoken words. The doctors cannot see it. Nobody else can see it. But I can feel it. I know it's there. It exists with the only purpose of driving me crazy. A rug growing from the roof of my mouth tickles my tongue.

 -random journal entry

DINNER DATE

"Please eat it. If you don't…"

Kayla stared into her plate, through the intertwined, long strings of boiled spaghetti covered with red sauce. Thoughtlessly, she poked at the food. The fork, plastic which was of not much use rather than a feeding tool, scraped through the top layers of Bolognese, revealing strands of hair.

"I hate to be rude," she said, "but I don't feel too well. Maybe I should head home."

"I worked so hard on this dinner," Freddy said, not trying to hide the disappointment in his voice. "Maybe if you'd eat, you'd feel better. It's not every day that I spend time in a kitchen trying to impress a woman."

A few months ago, when she met Freddy in a random online cooking group, she instantly fell in love with his monochrome photo. The shading highlighted his chiseled bone structure and darkened his brown eyes and hair. Even the dominant cleft in his chin added to his unique look, contributing to his cuteness factor.

It was a recipe for Bolognese that got them

chatting.

How they were both fascinated with the idea of combining pork, veal, and beef as the protein of the sauce.

The next thing they knew, they spent hours chatting via social media until they eventually exchanged phone numbers and often texted and eventually spoke and got to actually hear the sound of each other's voice.

Freddy cleared his throat. "I agree, three meats in the sauce doesn't sound appealing, but it's worth a shot. Don't you remember? This was the recipe that got you talking to me."

Kayla remembered, and a shiver gave her goosebumps, wondering if he could read her mind because that was exactly what she was thinking about at that very moment.

They had spoken for months but had only met each other twice at a coffee shop before Freddy invited her to his home for a dinner date with the promise of a surprise.

It went against Kayla's nature to be rude, and she wasn't sure the best way to approach the fact that there was hair in her food. Long hair. Blonde. His hair was dark and short. Where did this hair even come from?

Reaching for her wine glass, she took a long gulp of her pinot grigio hoping it would buy her a few moments to come up with an excuse to leave. Everything had been going great with Freddy until now. Until the mysterious hair layered on top of her food.

Freddy took a bite of his spaghetti, and Kayla couldn't help but notice that she didn't see any of the hair in his food.

"It's not bad if I say so myself. I think the veal compliments the other meats."

"Yeah, I'm sure it's great, but I should just go," Kayla said, now standing and hoping this wouldn't ruin her chances of getting to know Freddy better. "If I'm feeling better tomorrow, maybe we can do something?"

Freddy raised his eyes to her. "I really wish you'd eat with me now. At the risk of sounding like a helpless romantic, I'd love to spend more time with you. Is it too soon to say that I can see a future with you?"

The smile that grew on Kayla's face was genuine, and her heart beat faster. Butterflies fluttered inside of her, stirring up emotions. The way his eyes sparkled in person, something she never experienced with his online photos, practically took her breath away.

"I like you, too," she replied, and sat back down in the chair. "I'll just come out and say it then."

"Come out and say what? I know this is new, but shouldn't we be comfortable with each other? Say anything, please."

Using her fork, she picked into the sauce, dragging some of the hair above the food. "I don't mean to be rude but…". Kayla stopped speaking, hoping and wishing that Freddy would get the hint. If he had seen the hair, maybe he would have understood her hesitation.

"Oh. That."

Kayla waited for him to continue, but he didn't. Her date sat silently and looked through her, giving her the feeling that he was looking at something behind her. When she looked over her shoulder, she saw nothing unusual.

To fill the uncomfortable silence, Kayla spoke. "Did you order this from somewhere, maybe we should let them know their cooks need to wear a hairnet."

Freddy continued to eat. "I made it myself. I thought it would make tonight special. A home-cooked meal."

Kayla wanted to ask where the feminine hair came from, but she opened her mouth only to close it again.

"I really wish you'd eat with me," Freddy repeated. "We get along so great, and it might be weird that we met on the internet, but imagine if we ever had children, we could cook Bolognese for them and tell them that recipe brought us together."

The thought was sweet, but Kayla couldn't help but wonder if he expected her to pick the mysterious hair from her food and then eat it. "I guess I've just lost my appetite. The wine is excellent, though," she said as she brought the glass to her lips.

"It would make this much easier if you ate it."

Up until this point, things had been going great with Freddy. But the absurdity of this made Kayla shake her head. The reason it took them so long to meet in person after months of chatting online and texting and talking on the phone was because she was aware of the dangers of meeting people off the internet.

Kayla felt they had gotten to know each other well enough that Freddy was a normal guy, lonely like herself. Up until this point, there were no red flags and that made her think he would be anything but a great boyfriend.

She picked up her plastic fork and started to remove the hair from her food, only to realize there were many more strands buried deeper in the spaghetti. The thought of putting this food anywhere near her mouth made her gag.

It didn't matter that she remembered how he texted her daily to wish her a good morning.

Even thinking of all of Freddy's good qualities couldn't make herself force the food down her gullet. His eyes were dreamy, and he was sweet and even sent her random heart emojis almost every day to let her know he was thinking about her. When she was stressed out, he listened patiently, never interrupted her, and became her safe space to vent about life.

"Please don't remove the hair. It's there for flavor."

It took Kayla a moment to make sense of his absurd words. If there was any sense to be made of them. "You want me to eat the hair?"

"Of course," Freddy replied, still eating his hair-free spaghetti. "It really would mean a lot to me."

Kayla couldn't help but recall a conversation she'd previously had with him, and he told her dozens of jokes to cheer her up after a bad day. Mostly one-liners, but funny nonetheless.

His sense of humor was something Freddy was proud of. "Oh!" she exclaimed. "This is a joke, right? A prank to see how I'd respond? I can laugh about it, I suppose." But her laughter was forced and felt inappropriate for his somber facial expression and frown.

"Please eat it. I hate repeating myself."

Kayla stood, very uncomfortable, and just wanted to leave. "I don't feel well. I should head out."

Freddy stood suddenly and slammed his hand down on the table, which caused the glass plates to clatter. "Okay. You should remember that I tried to do this the easy way."

Kayla turned to leave, and a rush of panic made her spine shiver.

Freddy grabbed her by her hair and pulled her body backward.

The last thing she felt was a small pinch on the side of her neck.

A needle.

An injection that would practically put her to sleep instantly.

THE MORNING AFTER THE DINNER DATE

This was not a section of Freddy's home that she had ever seen.

There was a chill in the air and the walls were plain and white. The lack of windows gave the room a feeling of gloom.

Kayla raised her head from her pillow and took in her surroundings, trying to remember what happened the night before. Her memory was hazy, and she wasn't thinking clearly.

The twin-sized bed where she laid was comfortable, but not something she had any recollection of climbing into.

Other than the bed, there was nothing but a five-gallon plastic bucket in the corner of the small room, and a single lightbulb dangled from the ceiling.

It was a relief that she was still wearing her

own clothes, and none of her feminine areas felt painful or violated.

When Kayla sat up and threw her legs over the side of the mattress, a thick chain rattled as it pulled across the concrete floor. The weight of a heavy metal shackle attached to her left ankle made her leg feel too bulky and unnatural.

Her heart began to beat too quickly and her lungs couldn't retrieve air.

There was one wall with seams, shadowing the shape of a door, and she quickly ran towards it, only to find that her ankle chain was too short and that she couldn't reach it.

Also, there was no door knob and Kayla thought her eyes were deceiving her. Why wouldn't a door have a way to open it?

Reaching out her arms, the tips of her fingers could barely graze the lines in the wall, confirming her suspicion that it was a door. A section of wall that had the ability to open, but not from the side of the small room that held her captive.

"Hello! Help me!" she screamed aloud with a trembling voice, before realizing that someone had gone to great lengths to put her in this room, shackle her ankle to a chain in the wall, and not give her enough slack to reach the knobless door.

Who was she screaming to for help? Whoever put her here would likely not save her.

Then she bent down and used both hands to tug and yank at the shackle on her ankle, only to find that there was no way she could remove the solid, circular piece of metal.

A small hole stared back at her, which she assumed was for a key, and would be her only path to freedom.

"Is someone there?" A mysterious feminine voice was muffled and sounded like they were speaking underwater.

"Hello!" Kayla cried out again, her voice stronger and louder this time.

"Shut up!" she heard a man yell as a gust of air smacked her in the face.

The knobless door had opened, and standing above her was Freddy, the outline of his silhouette dark in comparison to the bright lights behind him.

The stubble on his face gave him a rustic look, making him even more handsome than she remembered.

Kayla looked up, a confused look on her face. "Freddy, you have to help me!"

"I asked you to eat the spaghetti last night. You refused. You chose to do this the hard way. I wanted it to be different with you. You were the one that chose this."

The memories of last night's date flooded Kayla, and yet she still couldn't comprehend what was happening. "This is about me not eating the food?" she asked.

"Not the food. It's about you not eating what was in the food."

Freddy remained standing in the doorway, a fact

that wasn't lost on Kayla. He was out of her reach.

Kayla wondered whether she should apologize for not eating the hair, or should she scream and yell? A primal part of her brain kicked in, throwing out all logic. "Let me go! I just want to go home!"

"I cannot deal with you like this," Freddy stated calmly, with no evidence of remorse in his tone. "I will leave you alone to acclimate to your new reality, but I have rules here. I already told you last night, but I'll only say this once more. I don't like repeating myself. So listen and listen good. The first rule is that you do not speak to the other people through the walls."

The door closed, and once again, Kayla was alone in the small room, chained to the wall.

Freddy's words, that this was her new reality, caused her to hyperventilate and wonder how many other people Freddy held captive.

ONE ROOM OVER

"I've gathered you learned that you have a new neighbor," Freddy announced as he walked into the room. It looked the same as the room he had just left, the same as all the rooms in this basement.

This basement was in his actual house, the one where he lived. A room allotted to him to be a full-time caregiver. In what was called a household.

Not the house where he shared dinner with Kayla. That house was vacant, listed on the internet as being for sale, and being sold fully furnished. Freddy also knew that the house had no showings that night because the information came from the realtor.

It was a perfect setting that afforded him privacy with Kayla. One that even if she gave the address to one of her friends just in case she was never heard from again, even if they searched for her, that empty home wouldn't help them find her.

"You broke rule number one," Freddy continued.

"But-you-don't-understand," the woman's speech was hurried and spoken without a break in between the words, "I-can't-tell-if-what-I'm-seeing-and-hearing-is-real." She didn't try to move towards him, already aware that the chain around her ankle was too short.

"I understand," Freddy agreed. "I can barely understand what you're saying, but I understand. You've gone four full days without sleep. Still, there will be repercussions. And a room change."

The woman scratched at the crooks of her arms, her fingernails discolored and flakes of dry skin broke free from her body.

"Do you want your next dose?" he asked.

The woman nodded, her head moving up and down rapidly.

"I need to figure out a way to move you without sedating you, or we'll be starting all over again. Sedating you would technically be sleep. We're trying to see how long you can go without sleep. Maybe I need to move my Rapunzel girl. I'll have to ask about that."

The woman sat on the edge of the bed, her arm stretched out in front of her, decorated with several scars and fresh track marks from being poked with needles.

Her body shook involuntarily, with slight tremors.

Freddy took note that the plastic cup of water was now empty, but the paper plate with the ham sandwich had gone untouched. If she lost too much weight, his friend wouldn't be very happy.

At least her bucket was semi-clean. The smell of

urine, high amounts of ammonia, was something his olfactory senses had grown accustomed to. The term nose blindness was what he liked to call it. If any of his subjects had a bowel movement, that was a different story. A smell he could never get used to.

"First the punishment, then the treat," he said as he looked at her.

Her lips moved, but she didn't speak.

Freddy wanted to keep his distance from her because in her current state of being sleep-deprived, he knew that she was unpredictable.

He glanced at his watch and knew that his partner in crime would be unavailable for the next few hours. Meaning, he had a decision to make.

Typically, in this situation of having to inflict a punishment, he would take precautions to ensure his own safety since he would have to get near her to punish her.

Sedation was sleep (or close to it), and they were trying to see how long she could stay awake before suffering from exhaustion. Sedation was out of the question. But she also needed her dose because it was time for her dosage of methamphetamine.

For speaking when not allowed, the punishment was tongue removal.

A nearly impossible task by himself. If she could move her arms and legs about, he took a chance of getting injured. Using force wasn't something Freddy preferred, but it would be necessary in this case.

Without explaining himself because he doubted her comprehension level, Freddy left the room.

+++++

Freddy returned a few moments later, straightjacket in hand.

A tool he hated to use, but it would constrict the movement of her arms by binding them close to her body.

"Put this on, please," he asked nicely.

The woman took the item and inspected the thick canvas-like, leathery material. "How-do-I-do-this?"

He was pleased that she didn't question his authority, which made his job easier, and helped her guide her arms through the sleeves and then tightened them around her body.

"How-can-I-get-my-treat-in-this?"

This seemed to make her even more jittery, out of fear that she wouldn't soon get her next dose of dope.

Freddy spoke calmly. "The treat comes after the punishment. I promise you that I'll shoot you up in a few minutes. I just have to do this other thing first."

She didn't look pleased, but now Freddy wasn't as afraid of her and stood even closer to her. "It's okay. I'm just going to put some rope around your legs. This will be over very soon. I promise."

Once she was safely restrained, Freddy told her to

lie flat on the bed, and he jumped on top of her, his legs straddling her chest.

"No! No!" the woman screamed. "Not-again! Not-this!"

"Shh," Freddy whispered. "I'm not him. I hate to do this, but it's my job."

Freddy wanted this to be over, maybe even more than she did.

Freddy reached into his back pocket and spoke calmly.

"Stick out your tongue," he instructed. "Please stick out your tongue."

The woman didn't want to, but after he repeated the phrase several times and realized that he wasn't trying to rape her, she did as she was told.

Repeating himself made Freddy angry. Very angry. Still, he tried to be sympathetic to this woman. He couldn't imagine how bad and irrational she felt without any sleep for the past few days.

Getting her to stick out her tongue was the hard part.

Once it was out of her mouth, the process was easy, thanks to a tool provided to him. It resembled a cigar cutter, but the hole was wider and thicker, designed for the shape of a tongue.

All Freddy had to do then was squeeze, which would bring a razor towards the hole holding her tongue, which would cut it practically half in length.

It wasn't the sudden rush of blood that surprised

Freddy. It was the blob of meat that fell free from her mouth and bounced off the side of his arm, still warm and sticky, that caused his alarm.

Not only because he was startled by being touched by the removed portion of tongue, but also because it was protocol, Freddy quickly jumped off of her and flipped her over on her belly. So that she wouldn't choke on her own blood.

"There has to be a more humane way," Freddy said aloud, his words drowned out by the screams from his victim.

"It's okay. It's okay." Freddy realized he was once again repeating himself and closed his mouth.

Reaching into his pocket, Freddy pulled out a cup of liquid and unscrewed the lid. "Your treat is coming soon," he said, "I promise. Now I need you to dip your tongue in this. To stop the bleeding."

The woman was moaning and screaming, possibly even trying to speak, as her body convulsed within the bounds of the rope and straitjacket.

The promise of the dope got her attention, and somehow Freddy managed to dip her tongue into the cauterizing acid.

"I'm so sorry," he said. "Speaking to each other is against the rules. It's for my own safety. Maybe not fair in your case because I don't think you have full control of your faculties, but it's a rule I must abide by. I promise your dose is coming very soon."

After getting her situated, Freddy swore he saw her smile through her bloody lips when he injected her with the drugs.

THROUGH THE WALL

Kayla heard screams and the sounds haunted her.

Holding her hands over her ears couldn't block the sounds of the distant (yet felt very near) misery coming through the wall.

Was this what awaited her in the future?

Was Freddy going to torture her?

Why did he want her to eat hair?

Why did he lock her in this room with a shackle around her ankle?

There was no other option, so Kayla relieved her bladder into the large plastic bucket, the sounds of it splashing against the material far different from the splashes of a urine stream into the water of a toilet bowl.

The smell was her own, but she was stuck in this small room with the foul aroma.

Also, there was no toilet paper to wipe with and it left her feeling unclean.

It didn't hurt when she peed, and there was no soreness to make her think that Freddy had raped her.

Her body didn't feel as if it had been violated, and the fact that she was wearing her own clothes led her to believe that Freddy didn't even see her naked.

It took her a moment to realize it, but as she patted down her body, she realized that she wasn't wearing her bra. That had underwires in both cups.

If this were a movie on television, she could have used them to try and pry at the keyhole of her shackle. The small hole that seemed to mock her, depriving her of freedom. Unfortunately, she had no clue how to pick a lock. Now she did feel violated thinking about Freddy fondling her breasts.

How could a man so handsome and charming turn into such a monster?

Her mind was racing with thoughts, and there was no logic here.

Kayla took a deep breath and took an inventory of the items available to her. No shoes, a pair of black leggings, thong panties (red and lacy because she was on a date that could have led to sex), and a blouse.

Her earrings had been removed, even her ring that had been gifted to her by her mother. One of her most prized possessions. 14K gold with a beautiful princess-cut emerald. Her birthstone.

Making her a Gemini.

Something she never put too much stock in, but

her mother had always believed in the accuracy of zodiac signs. Her mother had always bragged of Kayla's curious and intelligent nature. How Kayla possessed the ability to be quiet when necessary, but also be blessed with the gift of gab and practically be able to talk anyone into anything.

'Geminis are versatile,' Kayla heard her mother's voice. *'Sometimes moody and impulsive, but quick-witted and adaptable to any situation.'*

Kayla badly missed her mother, and had for several years now, since she had passed away during Kayla's first year of college. These thoughts were ones she had to push away, knowing she had to concentrate and get out of this mess.

Thinking of her mother was not helpful, so she continued to inventory the items available to her.

The plastic bucket was stinking of her urine. Could she throw the urine in his face as a weapon? Even if she did, she would still be chained to the wall. There were two small holes around the rim that she assumed used to house a metal carrying handle.

A mattress, not like the kind she usually slept on. This one didn't have springs or coils. It had some sort of coating around it, something she assumed was waterproof. Possibly vinyl. Was it full of foam? The substance within it was soft to the touch.

A pillow, similarly fashioned as the mattress.

And a sheet. One single, thin sheet.

Even if any of these things could be used as weapons, it wouldn't remove her shackle.

A shackle that was wrapped so tightly around her ankle that she would either need a key, or to cut off her foot to remove.

The thick chain could be a weapon. She could imagine using the chain as a weapon, choking Freddy's neck with it, but what good would that do? Unless he had the key on his person.

Could she risk fighting Freddy and hoping the key she needed was in his pocket?

The sounds she heard through the wall made her shudder and promised herself that she would fight if he tried to harm her.

The most hopeful weapon she had was her mind and her voice.

Could she talk to Freddy when (and IF) he came back?

How many women were here with her?

There was a rule, one he gave her as a warning, to not speak to anyone through the walls.

Then she looked up and saw the dangling lightbulb.

Glass. When broken, sharp and could be used as a weapon. A small weapon at that, but could maybe be better than nothing.

ENTER CALEB

I try my hardest to be helpful. To help these people. But in my dreams, when I sleep, my nightmares. Is watching worse than experiencing? I sometimes feel as if I'm suffering their symptoms. I wake with the feeling that I'm the one on which these experiments are being performed. I sometimes can't shake it. Maybe it's best to avoid sleep for a while.

-random journal entry

DAYTIME REPORTS

"How did that humanity thing work out for you? Or what was the word you used? Compassion?" Caleb asked mockingly. "I see she's here. The end result was the same."

Freddy stared at the screens, black and white, live footage streaming from cameras hidden in the lightbulbs of the various rooms. "I tried. I tried my best. What else can I say?"

"I warned you. You should've stuck with the way we do things. People from homeless camps. Drug addicts. People who won't be missed. I'm glad you took my advice and used a fake last name and social media profile. You've deleted it now, right?"

Nodding slowly, Freddy couldn't hide the shame in his eyes.

"I told you," Caleb continued, "you'd never get a girl to fall in love with you and be able to feed her hair."

"But she's a long-term one," Freddy protested. "I

thought it would help make things easier. I did-I do- actually kind of like her."

"Did I miss anything else today?"

"Yeah." Freddy took in a gulp of air so large that he felt his throat expand like he was choking on his words before he even said them. "Sleep girl. Was talking through the walls."

Caleb rubbed his hands together, a sinister smile on his face. "I get to extract her tongue?"

"These rules are for our safety, and I was left here alone with them today. I already did it, but obviously couldn't sedate her due to her specific experiment. It wasn't pretty. Not fair to her at all. Why don't we soundproof the rooms or something?"

"Because it's more fun this way, and that costs money, eating into our profits. For someone to have such a high-security clearance, you sure are dumb sometimes."

The two men had worked together, very closely, for over a year now, but their differences came between them on more than one occasion. Freddy hated removing tongues, but Caleb seemed to enjoy it.

"It's called a job. I don't understand why you're still here if you hate it so much. Look at the bigger picture. The good we're doing."

That was a reality that Freddy had struggled with. This was his job. A very hush-hush job, something so secretive that it changed how he viewed himself as a person. Unfortunately, this wasn't the type of job that you could put in a two-week notice and leave very easily.

Freddy wasn't exactly sure what happened to the people who decided to quit this job, but he feared the ex-employees ended up on the wrong side of the experiments.

"I see you're sad," Caleb said, hunched over the screens, closely eyeballing the girl who hadn't slept in days. "This is for science. The betterment of science. The more we learn, the more the doctors can do their thing and help others. The good of the many and whatever."

"Kayla hasn't eaten today. I'll try again later with her. Now that I think about it, none of them have eaten." It was easier for Freddy to switch back into work mode than it was to dwell on the things that he couldn't change. Feeding these people was part of his job and he genuinely felt bad for forgetting, but after removing a tongue, his mind had wandered elsewhere.

"I'll take care of the meth head," Caleb offered. "She sometimes eats, right? I need to get a good look at her tongue and see how she's adjusting. Can you take care of the hair girl, cotton ball, and piss girl?" Caleb scratched his head. "Are only four rooms full? I bet we'll get a bunch of new contracts soon."

Freddy wanted to scream at his co-worker until he was red in the face and remind him that these people had names. Kayla had a name and it wasn't hair girl. The others did too, but he hadn't developed a relationship with them like he had with Kayla. "Yeah, I'll tend to them."

"Keep up the good work," Caleb said with a wink and left the room.

LET'S DO A DEAL

Freddy knew he had better things to do, one of them being to feed Kayla, and that thought stayed at the front of his mind. But he couldn't pull his eyes away from the monitors. There wasn't any audio, but the grainy visual showed him all that he needed to know.

++++++

The woman deprived of sleep had the nub of her tongue stuck out of her mouth, resting loosely on the lower lip of her open mouth. The lump was small and obviously looked deformed, but it wasn't anything that Caleb hadn't seen before.

If he were being honest with himself, the mass of lumpy red cells intrigued him. The way the cauterizing acid destroyed healthy tissue, and still stopped bleeding by sealing off blood vessels, amazed him. The coagulation process fascinated him.

The way the human body could mimic healing

when offered the correct substances, yet still look so foreign. If it hadn't been in her mouth, he wouldn't have thought it resembled a tongue. It looked more like bloodied mucous clumped together haphazardly; like un-chewed kernels of corn growing from her mouth.

"You're not bleeding," Caleb said, more to himself, and did not respect a response. How could she speak without the muscular organ that was necessary to form words?

The woman made noises, the flap between her lips wiggling, and pulled her knees to her chest, trying to make herself appear smaller than she was.

The way she practically flung herself into the corner, the safety of a wall on both of her sides, was proof enough that she did not like visits from Caleb.

To calm her, Caleb searched for her name, coming up blank. Her name was unimportant to him. Maybe if he asked Freddy, he would have told him. Even if he knew her name, would it have been enough for her to welcome him with open arms?

The bucket of urine seemed to make the room feel smaller, the offending aroma worse than normal. Still, it wasn't anything he'd never smelled before. Maybe it was a sign of dehydration.

"Would you like some water?" Caleb asked.

The woman made noises to herself, not once making eye contact with him.

Caleb shrugged. "Well, I tried. Let's do this

anyway."

There was a bulge in the crotch of his pants, an automatic reaction from his body. There was something about a helpless female that automatically caused his blood to run hot.

The fact he could do anything to this woman and get away with it, the fact that he had done it many times before, only added to his erection.

"What if I offered you another dose?" he asked. "I'm supposed to stick with the suggested guidelines, but maybe if you're nice to me, I could give you something extra."

The woman moaned and groaned and scratched at the needle marks on her arms, and it wasn't until he promised her drugs that she glanced at him.

"Okay. Be nice to me, and I'll get you some dope. But only after."

The woman breathed deep and heavy, the air escaping around her extracted tongue making an odd whistling noise.

"Four minutes, maybe five tops. I need to feel that stump of a tongue around my cock."

She pulled the mutilated mass of tongue back inside her mouth and showed her teeth, crusty and yellow, like a feral animal.

Caleb expected this. "Fine. Have it your way. How about the dope first? Then you take care of me."

Reluctantly, the woman straightened her arm, in acceptance of his proposal.

The syringe was full and ready.

Caleb calmly sat down beside her on the bed, and her tense body language relaxed.

Her eyes rolled into the back of her head as he pushed down on the plunger.

WARM AND MOIST

Caleb had injected this woman several times, but he'd never seen her react in this way.

There was a layer of sweat on her skin so thick that it looked like she had stepped under a rain cloud. Her hand reached towards the center of her chest, and her body shook uncontrollably, gyrating the entire bed.

Calen wasn't sure what he was seeing, but he interpreted it as an opportunity.

Quickly, he unbuttoned his pants, shoved her flat, and knelt over her.

What he wanted was an extrasensory blowjob of a shortened tongue, the feeling of the small protuberance rotating around his shaft deep within her warm mouth.

If she was having a heart attack or a stroke or a seizure, he was well aware that his time with her would be cut short.

This was an experiment that would be easy to

replace. It wasn't hard to find drug addicts and deprive them of sleep to see how long it took them to perish within the required guidelines allotted. This particular girl had only been with them for less than a handful of days.

The portion of his mind that was focused on his job didn't worry him.

Caleb was more concerned about the length of time he had to achieve an orgasm.

The way her body convulsed made it harder for him to shove his penis into her mouth, but he was determined.

Her mouth was slightly open, which was more than enough for entry of his average-sized cock.

Now it was time for Caleb's eyes to roll in the back of his head.

Her movements added to the thrill of the many sensations tickling his sexual nerve endings. The heat of her mouth, the wetness from either her saliva or a freshly reopened wound, added extra layers of pleasure.

It went from one of the best blow jobs of his life to the worst pain he'd ever experienced so fast that his mind couldn't comprehend.

Her teeth had locked together, trapping his shaft in the tight grips of her jaw.

The woman smiled as blood leaked from the corners of her mouth.

His first instinct was to pull away, but found that only caused more pain but scraping his exposed flesh against the sharp points of her teeth.

Her body no longer jerked.

She was no longer gripping her chest.

Instead, she smiled, an acknowledgment that she had done this on purpose.

When she needed a breath, she opened her mouth and pulled away from her shocked attacker, blood spurting from his manly parts like a high-pressure fountain.

The chunk of meat she spit at him fell against his shirt, staining it with a mixture of both his and her blood.

Caleb was seeing it with his own eyes, but still couldn't comprehend that the tip of his sex organ now lay at his feet.

++++

The door behind Caleb opened.

"What were you thinking?" Freddy screamed. "You're bleeding! Her tongue is bleeding!"

"My dick! My dick!"

The woman's maniacal laughter filled the room.

Freddy rushed into action, already equipped with the cauterizing acid, in two separate sterile containers.

"Kate," Freddy said, "we need to stop your bleeding. You have to put your tongue to this. Same for you, Caleb, but with your....".

"No way, man!" he bent over to pick up what remained of his penis. "I'm getting this sewn back on!"

"You'll die before you make it to a hospital from way out here. There's no doctor due here for a couple of days. You'll bleed to death," Freddy warned him. "Do you want to live?"

Holding the stump of what remained, Caleb stuck the stub, what was left of his penis, in the container and Freddy looked away.

The fluid bubbled, a mixture of blood and acid separating like oil and water.

Caleb howled in pain.

Katie laughed louder.

Freddy was relieved. There was no worry now that Caleb would rape Kayla.

"That's going to leave a stain," Freddy said out loud and then closed his mouth, knowing Caleb would be more worried about not having a penis and not the discoloration of what remained of his shaft.

WHAT TO DO?

"Well, you're not bleeding to death," Freddy said.

"Yeah, but what's left of my dick is hurting like hell and the other part is in the fridge. Can they reattach it? I need an ambulance."

"Not here. You know the rules. Nothing to draw attention to this household. We're supposed to pretend to be a normal house out in the middle of nowhere. A bit off dick might make people ask questions."

"I'll drive to the hospital, then."

"That's over an hour away. And what will you tell them? How did this happen to you?" It took every bit of Freddy's willpower to not laugh at Caleb's situation but knew it was wise to stay on his good side. Not once did Freddy even ask why he would treat the women the way he does.

"That my girlfriend had a seizure while we were getting busy."

"Seizure? As in epilepsy? Then why wouldn't she come to the hospital with you? They'd still ask questions. Do you want that?"

Caleb thought long and hard and hated to admit

it, but his co-worker was making perfect sense. If he were to chance drawing any attention to himself, their employer might frown upon that. Part of the job requirement was to appear as a law-abiding citizen.

But how was this fair? Caleb was a victim. A dickless victim, but still a victim. Oral sex wasn't illegal, but there was a small chance the doctor might assume there was some level of rape involved if the woman felt the need to bite down and rip the dangling appendage from his body.

"It hurts so bad!" Caleb screamed.

Freddy wished that Caleb would put on pants, but couldn't help but stare at the broken-off section of penis and wonder if it the girth had shrunk in size because his was way bigger. The removed portion was merely a blob of misshaped meat.

When they had put the detached portion on ice, the flesh surrounding the head had lost its elasticity and looked like it was unraveling.

"I'll call one of our doctors. See what they suggest," Freddy offered.

"Yeah, either Santos or Garcia. They're both cool and laid back. I know for a fact that Santos treats women the same way that I do. I've seen it on the monitors. And Garcia seems indifferent about it."

"You could thank me for saving your life. You were losing a ton of blood in there. What if you had bled to death?"

Caleb sighed. "Here it comes. You're holier than thou and have never used any of these people for your own pleasure. You're sitting over there on your high horse pretending to be better than me? What about me, man? Any sympathy at all?"

Freddy tried, but no, there wasn't the slightest bit of sympathy for Caleb anywhere in his body. If anything, Freddy was relieved and loved that this happened. It served Caleb right.

The only victim was Katie, the sleep-deprived drug addict who was being held against her will. With Caleb sexually assaulting her on top of everything else was just icing on the cake.

Freddy was glad that Katie fought back. When he had removed her tongue, it was his duty, and he hated doing it. While performing the unspeakable act (no pun intended), he couldn't associate her name with her. It was easier to not see her as human.

However, in this case, he could call her by name.

His sympathy was for Katie.

"I'll call the doc, then I have rounds to make. Are you good here?" Freddy asked.

"Bring me some of those painkillers, will ya? You wouldn't believe how bad this hurts."

I wish I had zippers built into my skin.

Maybe I could unzip it, strip it away and change into something new, fresh, clean, pure. Unwrap my skin, cleanse it, and reapply.

Or maybe I could unzip my wrists and watch the blood stream from my arms, without feeling the pain of a sharp knife puncturing the fragility of my flesh. One easy unzip, from wrist to elbow on the inside of my forearm.

Unzipped towards a peaceful death.
Or maybe even a fresh start.

-random journal entry

PART ONE: SOME FACTS OF IT

RATIONALE

Being alone in the room, chained to the wall, was driving Kayla crazy.

The sounds seeping through the walls only added to her madness. The screams she now heard also belonged to a male. Followed by a cackle of feminine pitch.

Whatever was happening nearby was enough to make Kayla curl up on her bed and cover her ears to quiet the sounds of pain.

Her ankle was sore from devoting the majority of her time to using her fingers to try and unlock the shackle. She must have twisted her leg into dozens of different angles to get a better look at the contraption that held her prisoner.

It started with the outermost layers of flesh chafed from the friction against the metal, but the more she fiddled with the device, pulling and tugging against the clasp, the deeper the irritation. Two fingernails snapped broken when she tried sticking them into the tiny keyhole.

It gave her something to do to pass her boredom; a purpose.

Other than staring at the white walls and ceiling, there was nothing to do.

Sleep was impossible, her heart wanting to pound out of her chest in a constant state of panic.

Relieving her bladder into the bucket wasn't only demoralizing and unhygienic, but also a bitter truth of her current reality. This was what she had been reduced to. Nothing more than some sort of prisoner, or an animal, forced to endure the stench of her bodily waste.

When her bowels had threatened to move, when her clenched stomach threatened to vomit up anything due to the sheer audacity of her nerves overacting, the bucket prevented both of those things from happening.

Mind over matter somehow had an impact on her bodily functions.

But she knew that wouldn't last. Couldn't last. Eventually, her bowels would have to be voided, no matter how dehumanizing. Maybe even if she didn't find a way to calm herself, her stomach might win and force her to upchuck its contents also.

Alone with her thoughts, all she could do was think. Plan. Plot. Meditate on her current future, and how she could convince the man she thought was so charming to free her.

++++++

After the screams through the wall had silenced, the door opened, causing Kayla to jump to her feet into a fighting stance.

A weak fighting stance, her legs not spaced out for balance, but her arms out in front of her, her hands open like claws, ready to attack anyone and scratch them the best she could if they tried to physically harm her.

It was Freddy's outline, once again hanging like a shadow in the doorway.

Fingers still before her like a wild animal ready to attack, Freddy stepped inside the room, and the door closed automatically, sliding into the wall. Judging by how much she had toyed with her chain earlier, Kayla knew that Freddy was still out of her reach.

"It's okay," Freddy said calmly. "It's just me."

His stance was relaxed, and it took her moments to even smell the warm food that he was bringing her. The mixture of the reek of her urine, and the pleasant aroma of the food tickling her stomach, was a confusing and offensive fragrance.

Freddy didn't attempt to enter the room yet, and his eyes searched her face for any sort of recognition.

His words, that it was *just* him, shook her for reasons unknown to her. Did that mean that there were other people here? Other people worse than him?

"I'd like to talk," he said. "I'd feel better if you sat

down. And ate this. You have to eat."

He held the paper plate out in front of him, and she couldn't discern much, other than some sort of red sauce through the plastic wrap.

Kayla weighed her options.

Stand and fight? Make him mad. Possibly be locked in this room forever.

Or obey?

Kayla did not want to obey, but she saw no other option that seemed viable.

Biting her tongue was the only way to keep herself quiet and not lash out at Freddy. There were many things she wanted to scream, wanted to call him, question him, but the still functioning rational part of her brain told her to resist.

The taste of her blood filled her mouth.

So she sat down on the edge of her bed, each hand gripping her knees, her unbroken fingernails scratching into her skin.

SETTING PARAMETERS

"You have to eat this," Freddy said, offering the plate to her. "You must."

Upon closer inspection, she realized it looked like last night's spaghetti. The sweet romantic meal that he supposedly created just for her and their date.

He sat next to her, his leg so close that it brushed hers, but his upper body turned sideways so that he was facing her. The paper plate was sitting on his lap, and he got to work peeling back the clear food wrapping.

Relaxing her mouth, Kayla released a breath she was well aware of that she had been holding, and allowed her tongue freedom to speak. "I just want to go home."

"Eating this will get you out of here."

Kayla eyed the food like it was something alien, like she'd never seen a plate of spaghetti before. Even more noticeable today were the thick curls of hair, nested atop the pasta and coated in the sauce like a hidden treasure.

Freddy slightly shifted his body and produced a plastic fork from the front pocket of his jeans.

The cleanliness of the fork was Kayla's last concern, and instead, she gripped it and wondered how much damage she could do to him physically with it as a weapon. Even if she could injure him, and maybe plunge it into his eye, she'd still be chained to the wall.

Still locked in this room.

Could she unlock her way to freedom with a plastic utensil? Probably not.

"I eat this, and you let me leave?" she asked.

"You have to eat a lot of that. Over time. And when you've eaten enough, yes, you'll leave here."

How did spaghetti, specially made with three meat Bolognese, earn her freedom?

"I'm sure you're a fine chef," Kayla squeaked. "All you want is for me to eat the food you cooked for me, then you'll let me go?"

"I'm not the one holding you here." Freddy's calm tone shifted suddenly to something of agitation. "If only you had eaten his last night, then you wouldn't even be here!"

Her body did want food, needed food, but the hair was unappealing, so she started to pick it out with the plastic fork. When she got one of the prongs under the hair, she lifted it from the plate, revealing some of the longest hair she'd ever seen in her life.

"I suggest slurping it, like spaghetti," Freddy suggested. "I should have brought some water. You have to consume the full length of it."

"The hair? You want me to eat the hair?"

Freddy nodded.

"Why?"

"You're serving a higher purpose here. I tried to get you to do it my way, and you refused. Now you're here, forced to do it this way."

The screams through the wall started again.

Freddy jumped up from the bed, and the door automatically opened for him, sliding out from the wall like a pocket door, or similar to a door of an elevator. "I'll leave you to it. You must eat the hair. I'll bring water later."

Kayla cried, her tears dripping onto the hairy spaghetti.

She barely heard the click of the door locking shut.

CALEB'S WRATH

High on painkillers, Caleb still felt the throbbing agony between his legs.

"Think you're smart?" he asked the girl he would only refer to as the sleepless female. She wasn't worthy of a name.

This thing, the person laughing maniacally, was no longer human but a wild animal who had already attacked and had to be put down. "You do know you're easily replaceable," he continued. "I don't need you. You needed me."

Luckily for him, he was out of her reach, proven by the fact that she lunged towards him the moment he entered the room, only to fall flat on her face when the chain around her leg ran out of length.

If she was injured, or if her absent tongue pained her, she showed no sign of it. Her only mission was to hurt the man that had assaulted her.

Kate stood and bared her parted teeth, her twice now cauterized nub of a tongue black and swollen.

Caleb raised his leg and kicked her, knocking her backward onto the bed. The movement of his thigh radiated pure agony across his pelvic region.

The girl was sleep deprived, but she wasn't tired and her reflexes kicked in.

Grabbing the heavy chain that bound her, Kate held a length of it before her like a shield. When Caleb jumped on top of her, the clanking of metal links against his chest snapped him back into focus.

The syringe was small, hidden in his cupped hand, but he pulled it out and stabbed it into the side of her neck, and pressed down on the plunger.

"Sleep. Once you sleep, you're useless here."

+++++

Freddy should have gone into the other room and should have saved the sleep-deprived woman. That would have been the noble thing to do. However, his acceptance of self-preservation nagged at him.

A warning internally coiled around his mind, a sense of danger.

Caleb was unpredictable and angry.

It was safer to check the camera and see what was happening inside the room before trying to be a hero.

He was already too late.

Kate appeared to be asleep, ruining her entire process.

On the next screen, he saw Kayla curled up on her bed, hands covering her ears. That was hard for him to watch.

If only Kayla would eat, then life would be much easier for her.

Slowly, Kayla pulled her hands from her ears once she realized the screams had gone quiet. And looked at her plate of hairy food.

+++++

Caleb preferred the silence.

His only goal was to hurt this woman and it was easier with her sleeping.

When she woke, she would feel real pain. Maybe it would also help to clarify her mind, which would only add impact to her realization of physical injury.

The insomnia process had deteriorated her mentally and physically.

Caleb wanted her to be fully aware after he was finished.

The lack of a penis may have stifled his sexual urges, but he was still full of testosterone and hate. Revenge was a never-ending cycle. He used her sexually, she bit off his cock. Now he would do the equivalent and then some to her.

Revenge wouldn't magically repair his sex organ, but it would feed his ego.

Not only had this woman not slept, she hadn't showered in days. Pumping her full of meth caused her body to sweat, tainting the crevices of her body with an extra layer of stench. Urinating in the bucket without the use of toilet paper added to the glorious aroma of feminine hormones.

This reminded Caleb of Napoleon and how he requested his wife not to bathe so that he could smell her naturally.

Caleb understood this now. If he still had a dick, it would have engorged with blood, based upon pure smell alone.

Kate's legs were spread before him, her lady parts on full display.

Days of stubble had accumulated in her groin, and Caleb was glad that the homeless drug addict had somehow found ways to shave her pubic region before becoming involved in their experiments.

His mind pondered this for a moment. If she had no home before coming here, how would she shave? In a gas station bathroom sink? Or was she selling her body for dope and the dealer allowed her to use his bathroom for hygienic reasons?

It didn't matter.

Having not much pubic hair meant that he had a clear view.

FEEDING CALEB'S EGO

As Caleb allowed his thumbs to explore the inner folds of her labia, gummy balls of ick collected against his thumbprints. Dirt, dead skin cells, and bodily juices. A thick goo that Caleb could only compare to boogers or sticky wax balls.

Her opening was tempting, so he plunged a finger inside of her only to find that she didn't react. She lay flat on her back, her chest rising and falling steadily. Silent.

The sedative had practically knocked her out instantly. How much sleep did her body require after days without it?

Caleb pulled his finger out of her hole, and it was covered in a thick mucus with an even more pungent odor, which he enjoyed.

Between thumb and index finger, he tightly grasped her right labia minora and appreciated its elasticity. Each time he pulled it away from her body, it recoiled back upon her vulva like a wrinkled rubberband.

One last time he plucked the inner thinner lip from her folds and stretched it towards himself, but didn't release it.

Instead, he kept it taut and used his other hand with the surgical scissors.

The stainless steel was pressed against her body, the blades of the scissors open, and when he squeezed his hand, the snip caused an abrupt stream of blood flow.

It took four times for him to open and close the blades until her labia minora was fully dismembered from her body.

Coppery smell mixed with her juices, the effect pleasing to him.

If he were kind, he could have cauterized this sensitive area but weighed the pros and cons. He did want her to live long enough to feel this when she woke up, and hoped she couldn't bleed to death via a missing pussy lip.

To even things up, he applied the same procedure to the other side, ensuring to cut as close to her body as humanly possible.

From both sides of her vaginal opening was a fountain of red fluid, some of it trying to pool inside her, creating the finest of barriers to her vaginal vestibule, urethra, and sex hole.

Caleb wished he still had his dick because even through his pain he had the urge to stick it inside of her. Wanted her life liquid to coat his phantom penis like a glove, proving his superiority.

This would make them fair and square. An eye for an eye type thing, but it still wasn't enough for Caleb.

All he wanted was for her to wake up to unbearable, unimaginable suffering.

Lying on the bed were the two removed pieces of womanly meat.

Caleb may not be able to have sex traditionally, but he still had a sort of primal urge to taste the female form.

Blood and all, he wanted to toss the pussy lips into his mouth and chew on them like bubblegum. He couldn't stop wondering how they tasted. Would it be like sucking on old pennies that had been soaking in a can of tuna? Would the thin skin and meat snap between his teeth, breaking down into tiny swallowable morsels?

Instead, he shoved them between the sleeping girl's facial lips, secretly hoping she wouldn't choke on them. Caleb did not want her to die yet.

A realization struck him.

This looked nowhere near as painful as his absent dick. Her non-reactions and steady breaths proof that she wasn't in pain.

And to him, that wasn't fair.

Not yet was she in pain.

But when she woke up, he'd be sure to be there and force her to endure suffering when she was lucid.

MAKING THE ROUNDS

Freddy sighed.

The sleepless girl would have to be replaced now, which wasn't that big of a deal. It was an easy contract, short term. Easy to start over. Easy to replace her.

Kayla was a different story. A long-term contract. To the current date, Kayla was his favorite asset.

He watched her on the screen.

Kayla was eating the spaghetti, but carefully picked the hair out of the sauce and looked around the room for somewhere to hide it.

Freddy watched as she placed the clump under her mattress.

Did she think he wasn't smart enough to look there?

She'd be here for a long time and he had time to fix her and teach her how things worked around here.

For the time being, he had other work to do.

+ + + + +

Freddy had to check on his other assets.

His least favorite was the one that Caleb referred to as piss girl, so he'd taken to doing the same.

But before her, he had to visit the one nicknamed cotton ball.

Bucket and other supplies in hand, Freddy made his way downstairs.

This asset had been with them for over a week and was somewhat obedient and well-trained. There was still a slight bit of purpling on her face, healing bruises, from Caleb beating her until she submitted to their requests.

The worst part of checking on her was having to speak to and question her, for science purposes.

"Hey," Freddy said as he entered the room. After seeing that she was curled up in a ball on her bed and reading, he wished he'd remembered to bring another book with him.

Caleb offered punishments.

Freddy offered rewards for good behavior. A small item like a book was better than nothing when faced with boredom.

"How's the book?" he asked.

"So good that I've read it twice," she replied in a melancholy tone.

"I tell you what, do what's expected of you, and I'll bring another one."

"No more horror, please," she said. "I'm scared enough being here."

Freddy could've kicked himself. Why hadn't he thought of that? Unfortunately, horror was what he read, and all that he had on hand. "Noted. You hungry?"

Her eyes could have cut him in two, the way she stared at him realizing the trick question.

"I have to ask, and you know I hate repeating myself. Are you hungry?"

"Very. But for real food." Fury within her words, her tone shifted depression into anger like a flip of a switch.

Freddy searched her face. Was she telling the truth? How hungry was she really? It was important for his job, but the only thing he could go on was what she told him.

"Guess what then. This time, you get ten cotton balls."

"What? It's usually five!"

"Don't blame me. Blame society. The stupid people who came up with that stupid fad diet. In the medical world, doctors need to know more about the subject, and it's impossible to find willing participants. Lucky you!"

"When will I get real food? I'll die if this is all I eat."

Freddy shook his head. "I'm not even sure if you'll die from this. That's what we're learning. Maybe you'll just get a blockage and require surgery. Our doctors are on call at all times. Eat these, and then

I'll find you something else to read."

"A blockage? Surgery? Then what? I don't want surgery. I want to go home!"

Freddy couldn't answer her question because he honestly didn't know what came next. All he knew was that once the assets left his safehouse, he never saw them again. For Kayla's sake, he hoped they were released to live long and full lives.

"Here," he pulled a bottle of water from his pocket. "You know the drill."

"And if I don't?" her words were sharp and harsh, but still she accepted the bottle.

"Then we don't need you here. Which is worse."

Opening her mouth as wide as she could, she popped in the first cotton ball, took a long drink of water, and gulped. Hard. Repeated the same process nine more times, then opened her mouth to prove it was empty.

"Good job. I'll try to find you something that's not horror to read." Freddy changed out the buckets, switching out the one with a layer of urine for the clean one. Before walking out, Freddy turned around and asked her a question. "You're really not hungry, are you? This is supposed to act as an appetite suppression."

The woman shook her head.

THE LEAST FAVORITE

Of all the assets, this next one had been one of his least favorites of all time. So many people had come and gone, and Freddy tried his best to view this as work. Just a job. After so many times, these people didn't even seem human to him.

That was why he chose to go a different route with Kayla. To try and find the humanity within himself. To prove to himself that he wasn't a monster.

Freddy felt better acknowledging the fact that if he didn't do this job, someone else would. The best he could do was try to be better than Caleb, which was setting the bar pretty low.

To Freddy's relief, he found that he did enjoy getting to know Kayla. There was still some good inside of him. If only she had eaten the hair then maybe she wouldn't be here. If only he tried harder to convince her, then maybe she wouldn't be locked in a room, forced to be here against her will.

It would be a hard task, but Freddy vowed to work on his relationship with Kayla and do everything in his power to make this experience the best he could for her.

Every single time that he visited piss girl, he dreaded it. This time didn't seem so bad knowing that he'd soon see Kayla again. Get to spend some time with her. Another chance to try and feed her the hair.

====

"I brought bread and crackers," Freddy said, entering the room. "You can have any dry food you want. Any requests? I'll make a list. Like a sweet cereal? Jerky?"

This woman's cheeks appeared sunken from weight loss since her stay here. "If I choose cereal, do I get milk?"

"No other liquids. Sorry." Freddy shrugged. There wasn't much he could do about it. His job was to make sure she stuck to her diet so that when the doctors saw her, they could evaluate her condition.

"I have a kid, you know. I need to get out of here. Please."

Each asset sounded the same after a while, and it got old. "I'm pretty sure you were found in a homeless camp. No child in sight. You were dirty, cold, and hungry. At least you get food here. And you have a roof over your head."

"But I'm chained to a wall and-"

"I'm sorry." Even Freddy wasn't sure if his apology was sincere, but he hoped it was. "You're doing great things for mankind. Something bigger than yourself."

Her hollow cheeks were also still purple from Caleb's hand. Freddy did not enjoy using violence, and a small part of him was relieved that he wasn't the one who had the duty of ensuring these women were obedient. Maybe working with Caleb wasn't all bad. His co-worker's anger and brutality did serve a purpose.

Still, he regretted removing Kate's tongue. But he did that to protect Kayla, to prevent her from speaking through the walls. A preventative measure to help Kayla

"Here," he sat the food on the bed next to her and offered her a clear bottle. "Sixteen ounces. That's all. It'll get you so much closer to getting out of here."

Considering she'd been here two days, and not had a single drop of water, this one was tougher than he anticipated. He peeked into her bucket. It was empty.

"You're crazy! You know that, right?"

"Drink up," he said again, hating that he was once again repeating himself. "You're scheduled to leave here in two days." He left off the part that hinged on the condition that she was still alive.

"To go where?"

"The doctor will take you."

"Where? Home?"

"I can't answer that." Not because he didn't want to, but because he didn't know. "This is for science. To see how long you can survive drinking only urine. A documented case study. I would offer you your own urine, but you haven't produced any output today." That was probably a bad sign that her kidneys were failing.

The woman had been harsh with her tongue but hadn't tried to exude any physical force against him. Not yet at least. He did notice that her voice was scratchy and not as strong as the last time he saw her.

The woman edged herself to the edge of her bed, took the bottle, unscrewed the lid, and started splashing it on Freddy.

Not only was Freddy now covered in piss, he also now needed to fill another bottle. It was a messy job, using a plastic bottle, bucket, and a funnel to pour the liquid into a smaller container to be drinkable.

Plus, he still had some paperwork to fill out to update the status of the cotton ball and urine experiment.

Also, there was still Kayla. He had to find a way to get her to eat the hair.

First, he needed a shower, and then check to see if Caleb was up to the task of forcing piss girl to drink.

PART TWO: IS IT STARTING TO MAKE SENSE?

Finally, ?Happy Time

"You wouldn't believe the day I had," Freddy said like he was defeated, and sat on the bed next to Kayla.

She scooted away from him, very aware of the weight around her ankle, what was holding her here. The man she thought she knew was so casual and seemed to ignore the fact that he was her captor.

"I've had piss thrown on me." Freddy continued. "My co-worker was seriously injured which puts more work on me, which is good for you, I suppose. But now I have to replace another asset because I guess Caleb isn't up to it."

Kayla sat frozen in time. Stunned that Freddy was talking to her like they had through the texts and messaging. The same way he spoke to her as he had on the few occasions that they had met in person. Like she wasn't chained to the wall. Trapped here.

Before she came here, he only told her that he worked in general healthcare and taking care of people. Freddy never used the word nursing home, but she had assumed it was something of the sort.

Since he was so hot and sweet, she never probed him about the specifics of his job. It wasn't money that interested her. His job was unimportant, or at least she thought.

The way he had discussed making sure people had food to eat and cleaning up after them.

Freddy had even complained about one coworker that he had described as his friend, yet also a reason why his job was unfulfilling.

Never in her wildest dreams would she have imagined that he chained women to walls and kept them locked into rooms and forced them to eat hair.

"What is this? Why are you doing this?" she asked.

"Listen because I hate repeating myself. Eat the hair. If you had eaten the hair on our date, if you had fallen in love with me, we could have shared meals together daily. That way you would have still eaten hair, but wouldn't have been stuck here. We could have been out in the world building our lives together."

Kayla knew it would be best to hide her frustrations and not get angry with him, not when he was calm and communicating with her, but controlling her temper was a very hard thing to do. She faked a smile. "Okay, then explain it to me. Why am I eating hair?"

"You didn't eat the hair," Freddy's calmness seemed to erode as he jumped to his feet, looking down at her. "I know you hid it under your bed. Eat the hair. It's that simple. It's an experiment To study the effects and symptoms of Rapunzel syndrome. Basically, clumps of hair that get stuck in your digestive system."

Kayla was annoyed at the madness, but refused to let it show through her facial expressions. "Why are you doing this experiment?"

"It's not me!" Freddy screamed.

She couldn't help but flinch.

"I'm sorry," he said.

The way his mood flipped so suddenly caused Kayla to almost lapse into an anxiety attack.

'I'm sorry," he repeated, rolling his eyes once he realized he had repeated himself. "I'm not doing this to you. I'm just doing my job. Meeting you online, and chatting with you, made me realize that I can still be happy. Before meeting you, I let my work consume me. Devour me. You can change that."

Weighing her options, Kayla realized it would be best to pry any information from Freddy while he was calm. "I liked you, too. A lot."

Her own words had betrayed her. Had Freddy noticed that she used the past tense of like, meaning she liked him at one point and not now?

"Good," Freddy's smile reached his eyes this time. A genuine form of happiness.

When sat back down next to her and reached for her, Kayla took his hand and intertwined her fingers with his. "Okay. If I eat the hair. Then what?"

"Then my job is easier. Our relationship is better. It's the first step to getting you out of here."

That sounded great to Kayla, the getting out of there part, but she dreaded to think what else happened after eating the hair. "First step? How many steps are there?"

"Does that mean you'll eat the hair? Also, you never told me what you thought of the spaghetti Bolognese I made for you." His hand squeezed hers tighter.

"It was so good," she lied. It was food. Subsistence she needed for strength. "Walk me through this. I eat the hair. Then what?"

"Eat it, and then I'll tell you more."

As much as she hated it, Kayla had some special requests about eating the hair. "Can we make it shorter?" she asked.

"Not my rule," he stated. "Must be at least three inches in length. I can measure it better, and make it as short as possible."

"It was longer than three inches the other night! Who makes these rules?"

"Hair sticks to hair. Made it look longer I guess. Not until you eat the hair will I answer your questions." Freddy was proud of his plan of how to get her to eat what her experiment required. One girl liked books, one girl behaved for drugs, and Kayla would do what was asked of her in exchange for information.

"Okay. I don't want to eat the hair. I don't want to chew it," she said and waited for a response. When he didn't reply, she made another suggestion. "Can I drink it? In a milkshake? Ice cream? Something like that?"

"Sure," Freddy's face beamed with joy. "As long as

you swallow it. I don't think it'll be as bad as you think. You're lucky you're not stuck here drinking piss." The mention of his other contract made him remember he still had to get sixteen ounces of urine down the other asset's throat. The clock was ticking on that one. Time sensitive.

Freddy raised his eyebrows. "Any other requests?"

Kayla wasn't sure. Did she have any other suggestions on the easiest way to eat hair? She shook her head.

"Great. I have a few more tasks to complete tonight. I'll be back shortly with a milkshake. Chocolate or vanilla? I have both."

"Either is fine." Kayla didn't think the flavor would make a huge difference. She was still going to drink hair.

When Freddy left the room, Kayla paid extra attention to the door. It didn't appear that he flipped a switch or pressed any buttons. Was it motion-activated?

JOB STUFF

Caleb was drunk by the time Freddy made his way back upstairs.

The house was normal on the outside. It looked like any other home on the outskirts of a secluded small town, buried within hundreds of acres of forestry. The kitchen, bathroom, and few bedrooms upstairs were handy and made his life feel somewhat normal.

Freddy was surprised to find Caleb in the kitchen. A bottle of whiskey in front of him.

"How are you feeling, man? I see you're wearing boxers now. Healing up okay?"

"My dick is gone. Well, in that fridge," he pointed across the room, "so I guess it still exists but isn't attached to me. How do you think I feel?"

"Okay. Got it. Do me a favor. Can you piss in a bottle for me? I hate pouring it from buckets."

"You want me to piss in a bottle?" Caleb lashed out. "Sure. Let me show you."

Standing in the center of the kitchen, Caleb held the bottle to his crotch, the plastic lip up to a lump of acid-burned flesh and clumps of congealed blood. His man parts now a short stump of carnage.

Caleb laughed as he released his bladder, and liquid shot from his damaged dick in all different directions like someone put their finger over a hose. "I can't even piss right! I'm broken!"

Freddy felt dumb not thinking about that aspect of the injury. "Well, you didn't bleed to death. You're still alive. We'll get one of our doctors here in the morning. Promise." He didn't bother asking if Caleb would clean up his own mess.

Freddy had so much to do but all he wanted to do was get back to Kayla. Get back to normalcy. Pick up their relationship where they left off.

Pissing in the bottle was Freddy's other option, but he knew he could probably only fill half the bottle. Not the full sixteen ounces mandated that piss girl consume.

Pride in his job was important to him, but if the piss girl got a few less ounces, nobody but him would ever know.

"If I piss in the bottle, would you make sure she drinks it?" Freddy felt bad not referring to piss girl by her name, but it was something he had to do to disassociate her from being a human. It was one way to tolerate his job. Piss girl was not like Kayla, someone he knew deserved a name.

This caused Caleb to smile and Freddy knew he was probably making a mistake. One thing that did make Freddy feel better was that piss girl's room was far enough away from Kayla that she wouldn't hear her screams if Caleb chose violence. Freddy knew that Caleb would choose violence.

+++++

Drunk on whiskey and high on painkillers, Caleb made his way to the basement, bottle of piss in hand. The stairs were difficult for him in his current intoxicated state, but he didn't care.

This was the type of contract that he loved. Making the assets do something that was demoralizing gave him the feeling of ultimate power and control. A reminder as to why people like him were needed for this job. In his opinion, Freddy was going soft. Too soft for his tastes.

But that was also a good thing. Meaning if assets had to be forced to do something, Caleb got to step in and do what he enjoyed most.

"You're going to drink this," Caleb announced as he entered the woman's room.

The way her brow wrinkled, the way her eyes squinted, the way the woman looked away from him was all the proof he needed that she feared him. Which pleased him very much.

"No." Her words didn't match her body language, the way she had hugged herself with her arms like that would be some type of shield against him.

A day or two ago, that single word would have been enough for him to wrap a hand around her throat and punch her face. Followed by him folding her body to suit his will, pulling down her pants, and having his way with her.

Without his dick, that felt unnecessary. Was this all that was left for him? Violence without sex? No physical gratification after subduing her?

The whiskey coursed through his body and he felt the need to piss again, even though it was quite painful to do so. Pissing on the assets always made him happy, but now he was ashamed to pull out his gored stump and reveal his disfigured member.

How would he ever be happy without his dick?

Caleb was angry about everything. All that was left was to kill this woman.

She attempted to stand as he neared her, but her dehydrated senses were laggy and slow.

Caleb wrapped both hands around her throat and squeezed.

Unlike all the other times, his cock didn't - couldn't because it was absent- get hard, and it felt like a waste.

"I'll kill that sleep girl! I swear!" he screamed."But I'll make her pay the piper first!"

Like a fish on land, piss girl's lips puckered and parted trying to suck oxygen into her body. Her arms were too weak to fight him off, even with him being tipsy.

He released and her form collapsed face down onto the bed as she rapidly took deep breaths.

CHEERS

Caleb shoved two fingers into piss girl's nostrils, a weak effort to force her mouth open so he could pour the bottle of piss down her throat. His index and middle fingers were wider than both of her nose openings.

So not only did the holes stretch to the larger size, but his angle was awkward, up and away from her face, allowing her to get some air through her nostrils. Pliable flesh pulled away from her face elongating and changing the shape of her snout.

She did open her mouth though, and Caleb used his free hand to pour the acrid liquid between her lips.

Struggling for air, most of the urine expelled outward like a mist cloud of bodily waste floating through the air.

Her throes of choking, and the way her body fought against Caleb reminded him of all the other women he had taken by force for sexual gratification.

"Don't look at me!" he screamed.

Drunk, angry, and disappointed in his lack of

manhood, Caleb dropped the bottle, spilling what was left on the woman's clothing.

Cradling his hands on either side of her cranium, fingers firmly gripped around her skull, Caleb used both thumbs and plunged them into the squishy tissue of her eyeballs.

Both sight orbs sunk backward and recessed into her skull.

Caleb pressed harder until he felt the globes explode and a milky white substance leaked from her eye sockets.

Not satisfied that this was enough, Caleb kept applying pressure to the pads of his thumbs until his thumbnails scratched into the sensitive flesh of her eyelids and the cornered eye ducts.

Blood and rolled samples of skin collected beneath his nails, a sight that made him smile.

The woman's weak arms flailed and attempted to push him away, but he was stronger, meaner, and was determined.

Minutes passed and Caleb could feel the tendons of his wrist bulge.

Once he was satisfied, he released his grip, flinging her head away from him.

Before leaving the room, he admired his handiwork and her tears of blood.

The woman's sobs were a delight and he left her alone with her pain and blindness.

ANSWERS FOR CONSUMPTIONS

Freddy presented the milkshake to Kayla, proud of himself that he was giving her something that she had specifically asked for. It was proof as to how much easier he could make her life.

"No straw?" she asked.

"No, you'll have to drink from the side of the plastic cup," he answered. "I thought hair would clog a straw. Drink up."

He also had a milkshake for him to drink, but his was without hair.

"So I drink this and you'll answer my questions?" This was madness to Kayla, all she wanted to do was scream and yell and cry and beat Freddy with her fists, however, that was very short-sighted on her part.

"Yes. Think of this as a date or something."

Kayla found that to be impossible, but knew it was best to placate him. She had always heard that you get more flies with sugar than vinegar, and if anything, Freddy was now a pesky fly.

A pesky fly that she hoped she could win over and trick him into giving her freedom back.

A repulsed look on her face (snarled lip, squished nose) Kayla turned up the plastic cup and took a drink. To her relief, she didn't feel anything like hair worming its way down her throat. "Why do I have to eat hair?"

"This one's easy," Freddy got excited and drank his shake. "A medical condition called Rapunzel Syndrome. Where people, mostly inadvertently eat hair, which turns into a trichobezoar- basically a blockage in their stomach or intestines."

"That didn't answer my question."

Freddy sat down next to her and slowed his thoughts. "Most people who get this disease, they don't even know they're eating their hair, I think. They do it without conscious intent. All I do is get the experiments. Not the exact reasons as to why it's being studied. I guess they're seeing how long it takes. Maybe how much hair has to be consumed. That type of stuff. It's for medicine and science."

"An experiment? I'm an experiment?"

Freddy raised two singers. "Two questions. Two gulps. That's our deal if you want answers."

Not wanting to, Kayla forced herself to take two more gulps, smaller gulps this time. Mentally, she swore she felt something tickle her uvula as she swallowed. The taste was good though, and she tried her best to keep her gag reflex in check.

"Yes. It's my job to acquire assets for experiments.

Yes, you are an asset. I even start the experiments, but most assets end up in a doctor's care for deeper research. For example, one lady here drinks piss, in what I guess is to see how long she can live without water and drinking urine. A controlled experiment. One girl eats cotton balls. One girl isn't allowed to sleep. I've seen it all here."

Kayla shuddered at the thought of drinking urine. Hair wasn't appealing, but this milkshake had to be better than drinking bodily waste. She looked to Freddy, who had now relaxed on the bed beside her, his leg brushed against hers.

So badly Kayla hoped he would continue talking without her having to drink a hairy milkshake.

But Freddy sat closed-lipped.

Her questions had to be thorough to keep him talking, but that didn't stop her frustration from showing. "If you can't answer my questions, then who do you work for? How'd you get involved in this? Why me? Why did you lure me here and pretend to like me? I thought we were dating! I can't believe I was falling for you!"

Freddy held up four fingers, signaling she had asked four questions, but one of them he wanted to answer. Was so glad that she asked him. He answered before she drank. "I do like you. A lot. I tried to conduct your experiment without dragging you here, but you just wouldn't eat the hair!"

There it was, his temper on full display. His body tensed up and a vein popped up in the center of his forehead.

The most beneficial thing Kayla heard was that Freddy liked her, and she hoped she could use that to her advantage somehow. Playing nice wouldn't be easy, but it was necessary.

Silently, Kayla weighed her options in her head.

Her mind was telling her to play nice.

But all she wanted to do was ball up her fist and punch Freddy square in his nose. His hand on her leg repulsed her.

Freddy leaned back on the wall, and gently laid his hand on her knee. "I'm sorry. I'm under a lot of stress."

The way he said it bewildered Kayla, as if he didn't recognize she was the one chained to a wall and drinking hair. As if her stress level wasn't high.

All she had to do was keep calm and play along with his madness. Waiting for Freddy to speak, she drank a few more small sips from the cup, her lips so close to the rim that she used it as a strainer to (hopefully) block hair.

It must have worked because Freddy started talking again. "I did a few years as military police and when I transitioned into civilian life, I became a police officer. Went undercover. Made some bad decisions. So bad that I could have possibly gone to prison, and some mobsters wanted me dead. I played both sides. I was offered an out. This job."

That really didn't answer Kayla's questions, but it also didn't matter to her. There was no way she could verify if it was true. All she could go on was what Freddy told her. Was Freddy the mastermind of these experiments? Was it military? Government? Illuminati? A cult? Evil doctors?

There were so many possibilities.

"I really want you to be a part of my life. Think of this as a way for us to get to know each other better. You're the first woman I've tried to share my life with since I started this job. I needed someone good, someone like you, in my life. All I want is to be happy."

MORNING LIGHTS?

Without windows, time was merely a concept. Kayla didn't know whether it was day or night.

All she knew to be fact was that she hadn't slept a wink.

Freddy, on the other hand, had cuddled his head into her lap and slept for what felt like an eternity.

It would have been a perfect opportunity for Kyla to strike.

To attack her captor would have been so easy.

However, that wouldn't have freed her from her chains. From this room. From this place.

While Freddy slept, she felt his pockets for any type of key, but found nothing,

The way Freddy felt relaxed enough to sleep around her was a good sign that her ploy was working. One step closer to her convincing him to free her. Acting as if she was still trying to work on building their new relationship.

Still, it was not an easy thing to do.

In her mind's eye, she could visualize herself

strangling him until he ceased to breathe. Or beating his face until it was an unrecognizable bloody pulp.

When the screams through the wall began, Freddy immediately sprang to his feet and rushed out of the room.

Leaving Kayla alone to wonder what was happening to the screaming woman.

+++++

Freddy watched the monitor (safely from another room).

Caleb was still seeking revenge against sleep girl.

++++

"This will hurt you more than it hurts me!" Caleb screamed. "Shame you can't see your pussy! Oh yeah, I cut off those little lips while you slept! I have a doctor coming to help me, but I guarantee that you don't!"

Caleb had waited all night for the sleep-deprived woman to wake. "You're awake and will feel every bit of this!"

The tongueless woman tried her best to cry for help but only sounds escaped her mouth.

"Yeah, I want you to scream!" he yelled at her.

While she slept, Caleb had taken it upon himself to tie her up, arms stretched above her head attached to the legs of the bed, and her ankles done the same to the foot of the bed.

Her spread legs displayed a mess of congealed blood, the absent labia minora now indentations of delicate meat trying to scab over.

Using a knife, Caleb scraped away the top layers of gore, not caring that the blade was also eating into the inner folds of her outer vaginal lips. Fresh blood wept from her body and the sounds she made escalated in both speed and volume.

Her swelled meat burned with heat and no matter how hard she tried to wiggle away, she couldn't escape his touch.

"See this?" Caleb asked, hoping she could hear him over her moans. "A simple household item."

The woman couldn't help herself and looked up at what he was showing her.

A simple salt shaker.

He unscrewed the lid and began to pour its contents into her wounds.

Small white grains collected on top of the blood like snowflakes falling upon a frozen-over pond.

The initial sting was enough to make her want to vomit.

Once he used his fingers to mash the biting substance deeper into her fresh cuts, her stomach began to convulse upchucking its contents upwards her esophagus.

A foamy substance leaked from her mouth, and she had to turn her head sideways to not choke.

Caleb wasn't aware that the clitoris was the most

sensitive part of a woman's anatomy, so it was dumb luck that he struck torture gold by poking at the small nub with the sharp point of the blade.

Thousands of her nerve endings radiated pain across her crotch.

"An eye for an eye!" he screamed. "A dick for a pussy!"

Caleb grabbed her swollen left labia major and pulled it away from her body, then began to use the knife to cut it away in haphazard and non-precise slashes.

The blood that emerged from these wounds was thicker and redder.

It didn't take long, and the next thing Caleb knew he was holding the slab of meat in his hand, relishing its pliable texture.

To even up the sides, he also cut away her fatty right lip.

And then left her alone to bleed.

+ + + + +

Freddy looked away from the screen and scurried from the room, knowing that he didn't want Caleb to catch him watching.

His co-worker had officially lost his mind, and Freddy didn't want to end up on the wrong side of his madness. And he also knew he would do whatever it took to keep Caleb away from Kayla.

MD+ 1 MINUS 1

"I wasn't scheduled until tomorrow," Doctor Santos said as Freddy greeted him at the front door. "Are any of the assets ready for me? I'd like to not only tend to Caleb but also to them. Two birds, one stone."

It wasn't until the doctor stepped through the door that another man came into view. A man that Freddy didn't recognize.

"Oh yeah, this is my colleague," Santos said nonchalantly like an afterthought.

"Hi," Freddy said, sticking his hand out for a handshake in greeting.

The man dressed in all black didn't reply.

"Pretend he isn't here," Santos said. "He's here to mostly observe."

Doctors ranked higher on the food chain than Freddy, so he didn't question him. Still, he felt uneasy. This was the first time that a doctor had ever brought a colleague into the house.

Also, this was the first time that Caleb suffered a serious injury that required care from a doctor.

Caleb wandered into the room, his shirt covered

in blood spatter. "I'm so glad it's you." Then his eyes fell on the other man. "Who the hell is that?"

"He's with me," Santos said smugly. "Are you currently bleeding? Why is your clothing still dirty?" The doctor's eyes went lower. "Why aren't you wearing pants?"

Caleb's shirt was long enough that it covered his groin area. "Because my dick is gone!"

"Gone?" Santos asked. "I suppose I wasn't given thorough information over the phone."

The man dressed in black smirked.

"No matter. Let's get you examined." Santo led his guest and Caleb into a bedroom.

++++

"I see," the doctor said and cleared his throat. "Where is the member?"

"Member?" Caleb asked.

"The penis. Yes. Where is it?"

"In the fridge."

The doctor covered his mouth with his hand and stared at the mangled stump. "Was it removed with a hacksaw? This is very messy."

"Teeth."

"Teeth?"

"Yeah, she bit me real good. Chomped down. Tore me up."

"Then? How'd you stop the bleeding? Why are the tattered ends of flesh covered with? This top layer?"

"See here?" The doctor looked at his guest. "It appears the wound wasn't cleaned before the chemical cauterization." Santos wasn't touching Caleb and pointed from a distance. "The red is, I assume, is old blood. The black edges may be where the acid was on the area for too long, or necrotic skin."

The guest spoke for the first time. "I don't want to look at it."

"Necrotic skin?" Caleb asked. "Speak English doc."

"Where the tissue is dying."

"Can you fix it?"

"No."

"No?"

"No. But my guest here has some questions."

The man dressed in black stepped forward, purposely keeping his eyes off the wound. "How'd she bite your dick?"

"What do you mean?" Caleb said frantically, overwhelmed by the doctor saying he couldn't fix it. "With her teeth. How else do you bite?"

"Look at me!" the man snapped with authority. "Can you bite my dick right now?"

"What? Why would I?"

"Well, I'm wearing pants. Making it impossible to bite my dick. Were you wearing pants with the asset? Why was your bare penis close enough to her mouth for her to bite it?"

Caleb looked to the doctor for a helpful answer. "Who is this guy? Just please, doc. You have to fix me."

The man dressed in black pulled a gun from the back of his waistband, aimed it at Caleb's head, and squeezed the trigger before Caleb could mutter a single word.

HEARING AND SEEING ARE SENSES

One moment Freddy was watching the assets.

Sleep girl appeared to be dead. There was zero movement on her monitor and her mattress was stained with a pool of blood between her legs.

Piss girl held her head in her hands, but when she moved them away, Freddy saw that her cheeks were painted with a fair amount of blood. Not enough to kill her, but enough for him to be alarmed for her health. She was already on the edge of dehydration. Blood loss couldn't help her condition.

The cotton ball girl was fine but she needed to be fed.

And Kayla had finally succumbed to sleep. His girlfriend looked so peaceful. Having spent the night with his head in her lap, he wished he was with her cuddling in bed.

That would have to wait until after the doctor left.

The next moment, he heard a loud bang that made him jump to his feet.

Freddy was well aware of the sound of a gunshot, and he was sure that was what it was.

His first thought was that Caleb had lost his mind and was on a murderous rampage. But did Caleb have a gun? There was a strong chance that he did.

Instead of running from the danger, Freddy ran towards it, in hopes that if it was Caleb shooting then maybe he could talk his friend down.

Sprinting down the hallway to make his way downstairs to ensure that Kayla was safe, an open door and a wall of red caught the corner of his eye.

If Caleb was headless, his brains now dripping from his cranium, then who pulled the trigger? The doctor? His guest?

Another gunshot echoed up the stairway.

If they were downstairs shooting, then Kayla was in danger.

Freddy made a quick stop in his bedroom, and used a four-digit pin to unlock his gun safe.

Another gunshot echoed up the stairway.

Why would the doctor kill the assets? Why was Caleb dead?

None of that mattered.

All that mattered was saving Kayla.

Freddy made his way downstairs.

BUH BYE KAYLA

It was a relief when the screaming through the walls stopped.

The female voice didn't use words, but she didn't have to. Her cries of agony were obvious. Something bad was happening on the other side of the wall.

A male voice, one that didn't sound like Freddy was even louder.

Kayla hoped it wasn't Freddy. Every fiber of her being hoped it wasn't Freddy. The man did abduct her, but he hadn't physically harmed her yet.

The male voice was screaming about revenge and even named off sexual body parts (dick, pussy) to make her think the woman was probably being raped.

Using her pillow, Kayla covered her head, specifically her ears, and didn't want to hear.

Once the screaming stopped, she couldn't help how tired she was and fell asleep against her better judgment.

A loud bang woke her, and she knew she hadn't slept for very long because she wasn't feeling particularly rested.

The loud bang was followed by silence which made her think that maybe she had a nightmare.

Another loud bang when she was fully alert was proof that it wasn't a dream, but her reality.

Still chained to the wall, and unable to reach the door, Kayla couldn't do anything but wait.

The mattress was thin and flimsy, but she picked it up and thought she could use it as a shield. If she were hearing bullets flying around, it wouldn't be much protection, but that and a plastic bucket (which had urine in it) was all that she had.

When the door opened, Kayla peeked around the edge of the mattress, hoping it was Freddy. Unless Freddy was now a gun-wielding maniac.

Two men she had never seen in her life entered, and Kayla stood frozen in time.

"Oh, she's a good one," the first man said.

The other man took a few quick, giant steps towards her and grabbed both of her arms.

The first man stuck a needle in the side of her neck, and Kayla's world went black.

NOT A SAVIOR

Pistol in hand, Freddy made his way downstairs.

"Put that weapon down. There's no need for that," Santos warned him. "I should have told you about Caleb. But he was a lost cause. We put him out of his misery."

The man dressed in black stood in the narrow hallway behind the doctor and raised his gun towards Freddy. "I'd listen to him if I were you."

"Why are you shooting down here?" Freddy asked, his weapon still at the ready.

"One girl had her eyes gouged out. Another that I think was already dead, but my colleague here is overzealous I'd say."

Freddy searched Santos' face for any deception. All he wanted to know was whether Kayla was safe, but walking past them in this narrow hallway was impossible. "The other two girls?"

"Sedated. You, and them, are getting relocated. This household is outdated. The walls aren't even soundproofed. This location was still removing tongues and using cauterizing acid."

Freddy did lower his weapon. "Well, when I

started working here, there was so much of it in stock. They told me this was the way things were done."

Santos nodded. "I know. Your new household is less than an hour's drive from here. Pack up what you can. You need to be retrained, in a more updated household that works under our new techniques."

"My assets?" Freddy asked. "Can I check on them?"

Santos raised an eyebrow. "Why? They're currently in a doctor's care. MIne."

Freddy shrugged, not wanting to inform the doctor that Kayla was his girlfriend and he wanted to be sure of her wellbeing.

"They're going to your next household. You'll see them soon enough. I'll give you the address. Pack up what you can in your car. If you are moving anything large, we'll send a truck for the rest of your things."

PART THREE: A NEW HOUSEHOLD

NEW CO-WORKERS

Freddy only grabbed his gun, clothing, and toiletries and rushed out the door.

The hour-long drive to his new job placement was nerve-racking, to say the least, but his only thoughts were of Kayla.

Caleb had ultimately been his friend, one that he didn't always see eye-to-eye with, but still a friend. In this lifestyle, friends were hard to come by.

Was he mourning Caleb? Freddy wasn't sure, but couldn't help but agree with the doctor that he had been put down to be put out of his misery.

The last fifteen minutes of his drive had been on a gravel road that deteriorated to a dirt path, and he wondered if the GPS had steered him in the wrong direction. Trees lined both sides of the path.

Once the house came into view, it reminded him of the home he had just left. Secluded, but well kept. If anyone were to ever stumble across it, they would assume that a family lived here that valued privacy.

It appeared to be a one-story house, but Freddy knew to expect an elaborate basement. One that was larger than the dwelling. The main purpose of these locations.

The white, wooden front door appeared new, and even though Freddy knew he would be living there, he raised his hand to knock. The doctor hadn't given him any keys.

A woman opened the door and eyed him. "Can I help you?"

Freddy looked behind him and realized he didn't see any other vehicles. Did he beat the doctor and the assets here?

The woman was dressed in a pair of grey sweatpants and a white t-shirt, her hair messy in a bun atop her head. Behind her was a television, turned to cartoons, and Freddy wondered once again if he was at the wrong address.

The woman appeared to be about his age, so it stood to reason that she might have children. She fit the bill for a housewife. No make-up, and despite her striking blue eyes, the black bags beneath them were proof that she didn't get enough sleep.

"I'm Freddy," he said, hoping she'd know him by name.

The woman crossed her arms. "Freddy? What can I do for you? Who are you looking for?"

It wasn't until then that Freddy realized he hadn't been given any other information. At a loss for words, Freddy just stood there frozen in time and space.

"If you're here to sell something, I'm not buying," the woman spat at him. "I don't take kindly to solicitors. I'm busy if you don't mind." She then gestured with her hand like she was shooing a bird away.

"I'm not a solicitor," he said calmly before the door slammed in his face.

As he walked back to his car, he pulled out his cellular phone, only to find it didn't have any service. How was he supposed to call the doctor and get the correct address if his phone didn't work out here? If the woman hadn't slammed the door on him, he would have asked for her wifi password but also didn't want to bother an unsuspecting citizen.

Freddy banged his hands against his steering wheel in frustration. He couldn't even pull up a map, so his only option was to return the same way from which he came.

"Kayla, I'll find you. I swear," he said aloud, the words offering him comfort.

Once he turned his car around, he was met by another vehicle; a white van.

Freddy couldn't help but laugh.

The doctor was here, so this had to be the right place.

The woman who answered the door must have been good at her job. She had him convinced that he was at the wrong location.

HOWDY

Freddy watched as the man dressed in black placed Kayla's body on a stretcher, and he was at peace knowing she was sleeping.

"Aimee is waiting for us," Santos said. "We have the assets handled. Why don't you go inside?"

"She shut me down," Freddy said. "I thought you gave me the wrong address."

"Dex, get a load of this. Your girl didn't let him in the household!"

The man dressed in black laughed but was quick to voice that Aimee wasn't his girl. "My girl! Nope. That one can't be tamed."

It was nice seeing the man dressed in black laugh. So far he had been sullen and solemn, and Freddy associated him with being the man who murdered his friend. Also, he now had a name. Dex.

The doctor and Dex weren't careful as they lowered the stretcher out of the vehicle, but Kayla didn't stir. Freddy tried to hide his disdain. "Let me help you with that," he offered.

"I'd rather do this than deal with Aimee," Dex said. "Come on. Let's go inside."

+ + + + + +

Aimme opened the door and sneered at Freddy. "Pretty to look at," she said, "but apparently not very smart."

"What was I supposed to say? It's not like I could say that I work here. What if I had the wrong address?"

"You're right, staring at me like a creep was a much better choice."

"A creep? Me? What'd I do?"

"It's what you didn't do," she said. "You gave me nothing to go on."

Freddy felt like an idiot. "I didn't want to blow my cover or something."

The other two men pushed the stretcher down a hallway, and Dex was laughing as they walked away. "What'd I say? She's feral. Show him his room, okay?"

The interior of the house was much more modern than Freddy's last household. The furniture was much newer, the kitchen cabinets and countertops had been recently replaced, and all of the appliances were stainless steel.

Aimee didn't speak as she led Freddy to his bedroom, which was much larger than his last one. It had a king-sized bed, a nightstand, a dresser, and a television.

"Two doors?" Freddy pointed. "A closet, and what else?"

"A bathroom, silly," Aimee teased. "Was your last household a barn or something?"

"I get my own bathroom?" Freddy was amazed at the size of the large bathtub/shower combo, toilet, and double-sink vanity.

"We all do."

"How many of us live here?"

"I guess it's just me and you now. Dex has a room here, but he doesn't stay too often."

"Is that a raindrop shower head and wall jets? I can get used to this."

"Oh, Freddy," Aimee sighed. "You're not hard to impress. Good thing you're easy on the eyes. A bit naive, but pretty to look at."

It was the first time he'd seen Aimee smile. The way she winked at him made him feel uncomfortable. "Wait til you see the rest of the house. I have a feeling that you're going to be very impressed."

All that Freddy wanted to see was Kayla's room and make sure that she was okay. "I'm up for a tour whenever you are."

"Okay. Let's do this then."

"Lead the way," Freddy held his arm out in front of him.

The way she wiggled when she walked gave Freddy the feeling that she wanted him to admire her female form, even if it was through a pair of sweatpants.

REGULAR TOUR

"I assume you know the upstairs is ours. The downstairs is for the assets."

Freddy nodded. "Some things don't change then. The monitor room?"

"Upstairs. Makes our lives easier that way," Aimee said as she opened the door next to Freddy's bedroom.

"Wow." It was all he could say. The picture quality on the large screens was very clear, not as grainy and small as he was accustomed to. Even the two chairs in the room were luxurious, with high backs, armrests, and plenty of padding.

Freddy's eyes found what he wanted. Kayla was sleeping in a bed, one that looked much more comfortable than her old one. Dex was in the process of moving cotton ball girl from the stretcher to the bed. He also spied two other assets, both female.

"These black screens?" Freddy asked. "Empty rooms? How many rooms do you have?"

"Twelve total. I hear we're one of the larger operations. The black screens," Aimee paused.

"We'll get to that later. Those are for personal use."

"Personal use? Downstairs?"

"C'mon, pretty boy," Amiee mocked him. "Let's see the rest of the house."

+ + + + +

When Dex passed them in the downstairs hallway, which wasn't narrow, he made it a point to smack Aimee's buttocks. "Okay, macho man," she flirted. "I have my eye on you."

Freddy didn't bother to ask about their relationship. Not only did he not care, but he was still focused on seeing Kayla, in person and not on a screen.

"Here's an empty room."

As Aimee walked in, Freddy noticed the doors also slid into the walls, the same as his old household, and were set on a motion detector. "So the doors are the same, I see."

"Are they?" Aimee asked, and quickly stepped out of the room.

The door closed behind her, and Freddy tried to follow, but the door didn't open. "Hey! I'm locked in!"

Aimee appeared moments later, a smirk on her face, holding up some sort of a plain card. "You need one of these for the doors to recognize you. Did you have that tech at your last household?"

"No. They were chained to the wall. We didn't need them."

"We still chain them, but not with actual chains. More like a cable. An uncuttable cable. It's just an extra precaution. Like a failsafe. Also, I couldn't hear you. Did you scream in there? Our rooms are fully soundproofed. I hear your last household didn't even have that feature."

"I didn't scream," Freddy said.

"I bet you screamed like a child!"

"I didn't scream! And I hate repeating myself!"

"Calm down, pretty manchild. It's called a sense of humor. Go buy yourself one."

The door reopened, and Freddy was also amazed that this room was twice the size of the old ones. Even the bed was larger, sat on a platform that was built into the floor. The mattress was thick and plush.

"A toilet?" he asked.

"Yeah. Even inmates have toilets. Stainless steel, built into the wall. Like in jail. Water drinking fountains on top. Was your last household a barn?"

"Buckets," he said. "I hated emptying those."

"Your household really needs some updating."

"My assets. Can I see them?" Freddy asked. "I hadn't administered breakfast yet."

"I'm sure the good doctor did. Those blank screens on the monitor. For personal use. Are you ready for that?"

Annoyed that he wouldn't see Kayla, Freddy followed Aimee.

Freddy wondered if he should disclose his relationship with Kayla. Or would that be frowned upon here?

THE GRAND TOUR

"Before we go there, you need to get really cool really quick."

"What does that mean?" Freddy asked, offended that she implied he wasn't cool. Whatever that meant.

"I hear your last household had some issues. Rape? Am I right? We don't rape our assets here. We treat them as valuable research equipment and they are tended to humanely."

Freddy was glad to learn he wouldn't have to worry about Kayla being raped, but once again, he was offended. "I'm not a rapist. I do take care of my assets. If you recall, I just asked to see them so I could make sure they got breakfast."

"Okay, you're not a rapist. But your household abided by old rules. Did you prevent any raping?"

"What was I supposed to do? It's not like the job came with a handbook. I only knew what my mentors told me. I never raped anyone. I hate repeating myself."

"Calm down. Anyway, we have freedom to do what we want here, just not with the assets. From what I hear, doctors get better information from healthier patients. Are you ready?"

"For what?" Freddy asked.

Aimee walked towards the door, which opened once it recognized her keycard, and she quickly pulled him inside so that the door could close behind him.

Instantly, Freddy knew why. The smell was enough for him to cover his mouth. Moans assaulted his ears.

"The doctors know about this, but see, this is not an asset. It's a hobby. As in allowed."

From the center of the ceiling hung what Freddy could only think of as a meat hook used in a slaughterhouse. But what was impaled on the hook was not an animal.

The body was human, but the gender was unrecognizable.

Freddy looked away.

"Aww, you are a manchild," Aimee teased.

So he looked back at the figure.

The hook started between the person's shoulders on the backside, and the sharp point of the hook exited the front of his chest. "How's he moaning? Or she? How's he still alive."

"Aww," Aimee pointed, "see here. I forced the hook through him with perfect placement to avoid vital organs. Like the heart."

The body dangled, arms slung forward and limp. Neck loose, chin scraping near the tip of the hook. The feet were not touching the ground.

What repulsed Freddy most was the lack of flesh.

Over half of the body, the left side of the chest, stomach, an arm, and a leg, had been skinned, the edges of the meat in tatters as if it were unraveled.

The face was void of all epidermis, traces of bone protruding through a slimy red surface.

As the person groaned, which sounded like bubbled moisture escaping the mouth, muscles tightened, revealing their definition through the slick exterior.

"How is he-," Freddy diverted his gaze to between the legs, "-I mean she - alive?" Freddy asked, hating that he was repeating himself.

"It's a he," Aimee said proudly.

Freddy looked again but saw a smooth crotch, the same he would compare to the likeness of a doll without genitals.

His eyes fell lower to a puddle of blood beneath the victim. A thinner mixture had separated to the top, and Freddy assumed it was urine, especially because there were a couple of turds mixed in with the substance.

"A he? Where's the…" Freddy let his words linger.

"Don't get me wrong, I like dick and balls as much as the next gal. But not every man is worthy of them. This bastard here had the nerve to cheat on me."

"Your ex cheated on you so you hung him up like

a piece of meat and skinned him?"

"With Dex's help, used a sander in this area," she used her hand to showcase where the penis and scrotum should have been. "One of those electronic ones. Didn't even cut it first. Just ground it down nice and flat, polished itself with all the blood. Pretty rad, right?"

Freddy did not think any of this was rad. This woman was psychotic, and she had access to Kayla.

He couldn't look at that area but then made the mistake of looking at the face. Really looked at the face.

Just red moisture covering bones, and the bloodshot whites of the eyes looked unproportionate. Too large. Surreal. "No eyelids?" he asked.

"He kept closing his eyes. I couldn't have that."

The door behind them opened, and Dex entered. "The noobie, what was his first reaction? I don't see any vomit. I had bets placed that you'd vomit."

"No, this one is impressive. I think he might fit in here."

Freddy hoped that he wouldn't.

"Dex has his own room, for carnal sin he calls it. You get your own too. What will you use yours for?" Aimee explained. "Are you one of us or not?"

"Yeah," Dex put his arm around Aimee. "We do this to blow off steam. But never do we harm an asset. We collect bodies anyway, why not do it for our pleasure?"

"And the doctors?" Freddy asked.

"They don't care. They like it that we do this, so we don't have that urge to harm their valued assets."

"Want to see my room?" Dex asked.

Dex's Room? Initiation

"Co-workers make the best friends, right?" Dex asked. "We know none of us are narcs. You are an ex-cop though, right?"

"Feels like a lifetime ago," Freddy replied.

"Yeah, we all have our pasts. But now we're all on the other side of the law, but not entirely. Am I right? What we do, I guess is legal, but would you say it's ethical? We have the law on our side, or do we?"

"It's for the greater good," Freddy repeated, just like all the times he had said the same thing to the assets. Repeated words always tasted bitter to him.

"Yeah, but we're all some sort of messed up in the head. Otherwise, they wouldn't have recruited us, am I right?"

Aimee was silent and nodded as they walked towards Dex's room.

Freddy shrugged. All he wanted to do was see Kayla.

The door to Dex's room opened, and luckily there were no foul aromas or dreadful sights. Just a nude, unconscious female, chained to the wall; no bed.

"She's all yours," Dex said. "To do whatever you want. Show us what you're made of. We all have secrets. You already saw Aimee's."

"She's mine? Why would I want to do anything to

her?"

"She's showered and clean. I bet she's tight. You could rape her," Aimee chimed in.

"I told you. I'm not a raper!" Freddy's temper was starting to show, repeating himself once again.

"I don't think raper is a word," Aimee laughed. "Rapist. You're a rapist."

"I'm no rapist! And I don't have any grudges against any exes to mutilate!"

"Exes?" Dex asked.

"Yeah, her ex in the next room with the sanded-off cock and balls."

"That's what you told him?" Dex asked.

Aimee shrugged.

"Aren't you even curious about the sanding process?" Aimee asked. "We could demonstrate and show you how it's done. We need something from you here. Some sort of involvement. Some sort of secret."

Freddy's only secret was that he was romantically involved with Kayla, who he still hadn't seen, but he wasn't sure if he wanted to tell these psychos about that, not quite yet.

Dex left the room leaving Aimee and Freddy staring each other down in silence.

"I know your type," she finally said. "Pretty boy. You may not be a rapist, but from what I hear you don't prevent rape either. Dex will set you straight."

Dex returned with a large grin on his face. "Doc just left. I asked him to stay for the show, but he said he was behind schedule today."

Freddy was curious. "Santos does know about all of this? You weren't playing about that?"

"Why would we lie about that?" Dex shot back. Then he held up an item in his hand. It was about the size of a can of coffee, had a circular bottom, and a handle on the side. "Would you care for a demonstration?"

Freddy shrugged. His patience was wearing thin and all he wanted to do was speak to Kayla.

"Maybe we can convince him to rape her, eventually." Aimee was now the one smiling.

Freddy couldn't be sure if she was testing him, or if she was wanted some morbid rape show. "I'm not a raper!"

"Calm down, pretty boy," she cooed. "Let's get our juices flowing first. Then we'll see what we're all made of."

FLATNESS

The nude female woke with a jolt as Aimee bent her knees and placed one on each of her shoulders.

Dex knelt across the woman's legs, both of them using sheer force to pin her body down onto the cold floor.

"Pretty boy was curious about the sander," Aimee said to Dex. Her eyes landed on Freddy. "Do you want to rape her now, or after she's bloody?"

"I have a girlfriend!" Freddy screamed. "I'm not a raper!"

"Ready for the demonstration?" Dex asked.

Aimee nodded. "I bet he rapes her after she's good and messy."

Freddy turned to leave, but the closed door wouldn't open for him since he didn't have one of those special cards to unlock the door. His new co-workers may have seen this as a bonding process, but Freddy didn't want any involvement.

The sound that filled the room was similar to that of a blender, and the circular portion of the handheld tool that Dex held spun to life.

Dex pressed it against the woman's chest,

primarily the mounds of fatty tissue that were her breasts.

"Check this out!" Dex screamed louder than the tool. "See that nipple? A tiny bud."

Freddy didn't reply. He wanted to look away but he didn't.

From where Freddy was standing, he had a side view and watched as the breast tissue jiggled with the spinning motion and waved into the woman's armpits.

Aimee smirked as she held the woman down, unphased by the violence and the amount of blood that centrifugal force was swirling around the room, painting their skin and clothing in red.

The woman tried her best to get away from the pain, and her screams escalated. There was nowhere for her to go, proof that Aimee and Dex had done this before and displayed a perfect technique of restricting the woman's movements.

Dex turned the sander off, one of his eyes closed to prevent the flung blood on his eyebrow from dripping lower. Using both hands, he cupped her breasts together to the center of her chest. "One with a nipple, one without," he noted. "Which one does pretty boy prefer?"

Freddy couldn't help but purposely not look at the destroyed female form.

"Look at her!" Aimee screamed. "Trying not to get a boner? You could still rape her."

Dex used a finger to trace the circular outline of damaged flesh.

The absent nipple area was a tattered mess of ripped skin, leaking fluids, and abnormally flattened.

A puddle began to collect beneath the bleeding woman.

"I prefer this one," Dex said, marking her unblemished breast with blood. "To each their own."

"Yeah, I'm hot," Aimee said and then nodded.

Like they had done this before, Dex knew what that meant.

They both stood at the same time, stepping away from the writhing woman, away from the area her short chain could reach.

The screaming woman sat up, hugged her body with her arms, and started rocking back and forth.

Aimee and Dex both stripped out of their dirty clothes, and their bodies met, his firm cock between her legs.

"Pretty boy, would you care to join us?" Aimee asked. "You can have me. Or him, if you please."

"No! I would never cheat on my Kayla!"

Dex ignored everything else and allowed his mouth to explore Aimee's body, his warm lips clamping onto her tit.

"You can have her if you want," Aimee continued. "We'd help you hold her down if you want."

"I do not want to be here! Let me out!"

Dex removed his mouth from Aimee's body. "Wrong answer, pretty boy. You know so much about us. We know nothing about you. What's your darkness?"

The last word threw Freddy for a loop. He didn't think he harbored any darkness. "Please, let me leave. I don't care what you do. I just want to see Kayla!"

Aimee pulled away from Dex, breaking the connection between their two bodies. "Kayla? Is that your girlfriend's name? Maybe he's not a rapist. Maybe he's okay. Dex, let the pretty boy out. Give us a few minutes, we have something real to show you."

Dex threw his shirt towards the door, and the key card in the pocket triggered the motion, allowing Freddy out into the hallway.

DEX'S REAL ROOM

Freddy could have kicked himself for saying Kayla's name. Would they question whether the hair-eating girl was his girlfriend? How would they feel about him being romantically involved with an asset?

Nothing could be heard in the hallway, but all he could assume was that Aimee and Dex wanted to be alone to either bang each other or talk privately.

There were so many other doors, and Freddy had no clue which one Kayla was behind, but it didn't matter without a keycard. He couldn't open any of the doors.

So he waited...

++++++

Two minutes later, both Dex and Aimee came out of the room, fully dressed but still covered in blood.

"We're not always this chaotic," Dex explained.

"You're a noobie and we wanted to get a feel for you. Getting to know people is difficult. We found these sorts of tactics work better."

"Yeah, you didn't rape the woman," Aimee chimed in. "You'd be surprised how many people would have, especially after she was bloodied."

The large void in Freddy's throat prevented him from bringing up Caleb. If Caleb hadn't been put out of his misery and brought to this household, he would have been all over the woman. "I don't appreciate mind games or tests or whatever."

"Good." Dex led them down the hall to yet another door. "I guess we can let you in on some of what we really do. In our downtime, of course. The assets always come first."

A door opened, and this room was set up like something out of a hospital. A surgical steel table in the center, what Freddy could only assume was a body beneath a sheet. Large equipment with flashing lights and a computer lined a wall. 'It's certainly clean in here. Much better than the past two rooms you showed me."

"If this job has taught me anything, it's how to get good at making people disappear," Aimee bragged. "We have fun learning here."

"Learning what?" Freddy asked.

"Anything we want," Dex answered as he pulled the sheet back revealing a sleeping man's face. "I have a hypothesis about something. Aimee wanted to see it come to life. So we do this sort of stuff."

"Vague much?" Freddy asked. "A hypothesis about what? What sort of stuff?"

"What do you think a transfusion of boiling blood would do to the human body?" Aimee asked. "Dex has his suspicions, but we're not completely sure."

"Why? Is this for the greater good?"

Dex shrugged. "Why not? Maybe. Maybe not. The greater good? You sound like some of the old-school mentors that brainwashed me when I started working here. Does everything need a reason? Does everything need a practical application?"

"How is this different from senseless violence?" Freddy defended his stance. "At least the assets are helping within the medical world."

"Maybe this will, too, someday. We don't know yet. It keeps me sane." Dex started tapping buttons on the computer.

Aimee watched in anticipation. "It's fun to think outside the box. You should try it sometime, pretty boy. It's better than letting women get raped."

"Don't rain on my parade," Dex warned. "I've already taken a few pints from him, so I'm sure the blood type is correct. The patient will be getting his own blood back, just at a couple hundred degrees Fahrenheit. Are we ready?"

Aimee swiped some smelling salts under the sleeping, restrained man's nostrils while Dex hooked up another machine and put a needle in the man's arm.

TORRID VITAL

"What the!?" the man screamed as he found his limbs were immobilized.

A monitor that Dex rolled beside the bed was showing a rapid heartbeat and elevated blood pressure. "Calm down. I want clear readings." Then he looked at Aimee. "Good call on adding a thicker, updated IV line. I'd hate to have melted one."

"You thought of everything." It was all Freddy could think to say, even if he didn't agree with what they were doing. This wasn't a random spur-of-the-moment experiment that his new co-workers threw together on a whim. "I hate to say that I'm impressed, but-". At a loss for more words, Freddy closed his mouth.

"Told you he'd fit in," Dex said to Aimee. "I'm glad we didn't get the rapist. That would get boring."

Freddy couldn't help but wonder what else they had been told about him and Caleb. Was the original plan for Caleb to come work here with them? Did Dex shoot Caleb because he didn't want him in this household? Did that mean Dex would murder him if they didn't like something about him?

Was Freddy in danger? Even more important, was Kayla in danger? What would they do if they figured out she was his girlfriend? Was there a way for him to even the playing field? There were two of them and only one of him, and this was their home turf.

Freddy was just the new guy.

"What are you doing to me? Stop this!"

Dex obviously wasn't happy with the patient because he frowned.

"Should I sedate him?" Aimee asked. "Not fully asleep, but calm him."

Freddy watched as Aimee grabbed a syringe from a cabinet, stuck the needle into a small vial, filled it, and shot it into the man's intravenous line. They were professional even if they were immoral.

The medicine seemed to calm the patient who stopped fighting against his restraints.

"Are we ready?" Dex asked.

The intricate tubes and lines running from monitors and machines were thorough, but all Freddy could focus on was the direct line into the man's arm, which was now flowing with fluid.

"The computer says it's not at the full boiling point." Dex shrugged. "Let's hope it's hot enough."

A steady, rhythmic beep came from the monitor. Which coordinated with the calm patient's heartbeat.

The dark fluid reached the IV entry point into the patient's arm and beeps became much quicker.

Freddy watched as lines on the screen zigged and zagged up and down.

"Mute the volume!" Dex screamed. "That beeping will drive me crazy!"

Aimee stepped forward and pushed a few buttons until it was silent.

What could be seen through the patient's arm skin was a purple marbling beneath.

A new smell lingered in the air that made Freddy remember that he skipped a meal and needed to eat. Not quite the aroma of cooked meat, but close enough.

Soon, the patient's fingers darkened, and Aimee touched one. "It is hot!"

The patient began to moan and his bloodshot eyes rolled backwards in a fluttering motion.

Skin tissue above the veins swelled like round lumps and traveled toward the man's torso. The entirety of the arm was flushed red.

"Heat stroke? Blood clots? The possibilities are endless!" Dex screamed. "But he's still alive!"

Aimee gasped. "But for how long?"

The lines on the screen became even more erratic and all of the numbers had practically doubled.

A white foamy substance expelled from the patient's mouth as his cheeks bloated and lined with spider cracks. The frontal veins of his forehead expanded causing wrinkling.

The arm, near the IV entry, now blackened. "He's being cooked from the inside out!" Aimee cheered.

Everything was happening so fast, yet Freddy felt

like he was watching in slow motion as skin tissue became damaged and discolored.

The man's chest rose and fell, struggling for breath, the foam of the mouth now thicker.

Blisters developed throughout the flesh, and the chest and arm skin looked like it was flaking, cracking away, shriveling in spots, and expanding in others.

Freddy looked away. "What is the purpose of this?"

"He's dead," Aimee gasped.

Dex looked at the computer screen. "The blood warmer, it got hotter. Why? It made the blood too hot! What'd I do wrong? I hoped he lived longer!"

"You set it wrong!" Aimee screamed. "Or maybe it was when you modified the machine! I knew you'd mess this up!"

Even though Freddy was no longer watching the destruction of this human body, the smell was something he could not ignore. A charcoal mixture of burnt hair and meat. "Can I use someone's keycard? I need to get out of here!"

"Poor pretty boy," Aimee snapped. "Can't run with the big dogs? Maybe you don't belong here with us."

All Freddy wanted to do was see Kayla and was relieved when Aimee opened the door for him.

Knowing he couldn't open Kayla's door even if he knew which room she was in, Freddy went upstairs to watch her from the camera.

PART FOUR: KEEPING COOL

NEW AND BETTER

Kayla felt the same as she had after dinner with Freddy, the effects of being drugged and groggy were very similar to a bad hangover.

Where she lay felt different, more comfortable, with more padding beneath her. There was even a fluffy pillow.

She glanced down to see that her clothing had been removed and replaced with a hospital gown. Her first thought was whether Freddy had raped her, but her last memory was of faces she didn't know. Had Freddy's co-worker raped her?

Fortunately, her lady parts didn't ache or feel like they had been violated.

The room felt as if it were spinning around her as she sat up.

Her bladder beckoned, and she swung her legs over the side of the bed, and her ankle felt lighter. The thick chain was now replaced with a thinner wire wrapped in some type of rubber barrier.

An angry bruise from the heavier chain still blemished her flesh and she was still connected to a wall but in a much more comfortable manner.

Mindlessly she sat on the toilet, and it took her moments to realize her plastic bucket had been upgraded.

Kayla scratched her head, wondering if she had dreamt all of it. Was this part of the torture? Was toying with her mind a part of her experiment? Or had Freddy done or said something to improve her living conditions?

In a million years Kayla would have never dreamt that she would be thankful for something as simple as a toilet and running water. If- no, when- she got free from this place she would never take a toilet for granted ever again.

After flushing, she took advantage of her seated position to thumb at her new type of shackle. More comfortable than a chain, but still seemed to be a lost cause. No matter how much she pried at it, it was too tight to roll down her foot and impossible to open.

A small part of her wanted to see Freddy. The man who jabbed her with the needle wasn't as friendly, and although Freddy was also her abductor, maybe he was her only chance of getting out of this place.

She had no plan, other than to play along with Freddy and hopefully convince him to let her leave. If she had to eat some hair here to appease him, then that's what she would have to do.

The screams she had heard through the walls the day before haunted her silent room. Was it possible to avoid Freddy's coworker somehow? Or had it been Freddy causing the woman in the next room to scream?

Did she believe Freddy when he said it hadn't been his doing?

Or was that another mind game? His lying would give her false hopes that he wasn't as bad as the other people in this prison.

How long had she been here? Who would be looking for her? If anything, people would be concerned when she didn't show up for work, but would they actively search for her? This was the first time in her life that she regretted not being very active socially.

Sure, she had friends, but she was the type of person that had very few real friends, but many online friends. Her real-life friends she didn't see often enough for them to be concerned after a few days of being missing.

It was hard to think through her drug-induced brain fog, and Kayla found comfort that she had shared details about Freddy in one of her online book clubs. It was a small chat comprised of three other women, where they'd read a book and discuss it once a month.

Three women who she'd never met in real life.

Three women who wouldn't be concerned until the end of the month when they all chatted about the book. Many times they chatted online sporadically throughout the month, but not often enough for them to be concerned about her.

Had she told anyone the exact details of her date with Freddy at his house? She thought she did, but now she was frail and not thinking straight. Even if any of her friends were searching for her, would they be able to find her?

AND FREDDY WATCHED

If only he had a keycard then Freddy could search for Kayla.

She was so close, close enough to see on the monitor, yet so far away. In one of the rooms downstairs, but he wasn't even sure which one.

Freddy watched as Kayla used the toilet, and he swore that he saw her smile. It appeared that she was enjoying her upgraded living conditions.

Freddy also saw the cotton ball girl, who was lying in bed, and two other people he didn't recognize. One male, and the other female. Curious as to what their experiments might be, Freddy punched buttons on the keyboard, but this computer system was nothing like the one he used in his last household.

What he did manage to do was pull up the camera views for what Dex and Aimee referred to as their personal rooms.

The man who was boiled from the inside out

with his own blood was still dead.

The hanging man, the one Aimee claimed was her ex, still dangled from a meat hook. Why had Dex acted surprised when Freddy referred to the man as Aimee's ex?

There was movement in the woman's room that Dex had used a sander to destroy her breast.

Dex entered, and Freddy raised an eyebrow, wondering what Dex had planned for her. Aimee seemed to be persistent about rape, and he wondered if that was what Dex was going to do to her.

Aimee was nowhere to be seen, giving Freddy the impression that there were blindspots from the cameras.

Freddy watched as Dex held something small, and sat on top of the crying woman's chest, pinning her down.

Dex delicately held one of the woman's hands in his own, and stretched out each of her fingers.

Then he ran whatever he held against her skin, scraping it off as it rolled against the tool and fell to the floor.

Freddy looked closer.

Dex was using a vegetable peeler to scrape away the top layers of her flesh, revealing the bones of her fingers with a mess of blood. What was the purpose of this? Why would they randomly torture people?

On the bright side, their other assets didn't seem to be maimed, which gave him hope that Kayla was safe.

"Like what you see?"

Freddy turned around to find Aimee, her hair damp from what he assumed a shower since her skin was free of blood spatter, watching him. "You've figured out how to view our rooms. Kudos to you, pretty boy."

"When do I get my keycard? And I also need to be briefed on the experiments. I'm ready to work."

Aimee held up a file. "Yeah, I did some digging myself. It looks like our Rapunzel girl is named Kayla. Is that a coincidence? Or are you in a relationship with an asset?"

Freddy searched Aimee's face, trying to find anything to hint at how she would feel about him being romantically involved with one of their experiments. "Wow. What a question. How about you answer this for me? What's Dex doing? Why is he skinning that woman's hand?"

Aimee shrugged. "Why not? I guess he's just seeing how much pain the human body can endure before going into shock and accepting her fate. She's as good as dead anyway. Today, we plan to dispose of some bodies. You want to work? That's your first task. Help us get rid of them."

"Them who?"

"Our toys. They'll stink up the place if we don't dispose of them. You do know that none of our assets live after their experiments, right? If Kayla is your girlfriend, she's dead too."

"What do you mean? Hypothetically, say that is

my Kayla. She'll eat hair until she gets a blockage, the doctors will do their surgery and save her."

Aimee laughed. "Then they kill her. Or reuse her in another experiment. Do you think they'd release her back into society so that she could tell the world what happened to her? It's a good thing you're easy on the eyes because you're not that smart."

Freddy's mouth fell open. Why did he assume they released the assets after they were done with them? Was this true? Did they kill them after their experiment? "That's not true."

"I don't care if you believe me or not." Aimee directed her attention towards the monitor. "Look, Dex is using the vegetable peeler up her arms now. This one's a fighter. True grit. Wants to live so badly. She's even trying to buck him off of her. It doesn't matter. Today is cleaning day. Are you ready?"

CLEANING HOUSE

By the time they made it into Dex's room, the woman was a bloody mess of peeled-away skin and blood. He had even used the vegetable peeler on her face, with careful attention paid to the curvature of her bone structure.

Especially around one of her eyes.

The woman's left eye had been botched, too much skin torn away in a jagged mess and thick chunks. A mangled blob of destruction encasing the sight organ.

However, her right eye had been precise, only the epidermis removed delicately. Thin layers of dermis scraped away showcasing what was buried beneath.

"I'm not finished!" Dex yelled.

"Yes, you are." Aimee looked at her wrist, and pointed, even though she wasn't wearing a watch. "We're on a schedule. You're almost out of time."

"Out of time? For what?" Freddy asked.

"My time is spent doing other jobs. This isn't my only household," Dex answered. "I'll have to be leaving soon."

"Exactly," Aimee pointed at the door. "Go get cleaned up. Say bye before you leave. I have pretty boy here to help me clean. He has to earn his keycard. For some reason, he wants it badly."

Dex didn't question her and obeyed. "I'll let you know before I leave."

The woman was still alive, but her screams were now faint and her breathing was heavy. "Good, she's still alive. I like it this way."

It now made sense as to why Aimme brought a gurney with them. "Help me pick her up and put her up here. You get the honor of picking up all the loose meat."

"Loose meat? What?" Freddy looked at the flecks of discarded human skin in disgust. "No way. I didn't sign up for this."

"Here," Aimee pulled a pair of disposable gloves and apron from beneath the gurney and threw them at him. "Put these on."

"I don't want to do this!"

"Do you want your keycard or not? How bad do you want to see Kayla?"

Freddy didn't want to answer because he didn't want to confirm or deny that his girlfriend was an asset. "Many people have the name Kayla, you are aware?"

"Um, hmm. We need to get her to the incinerator. Help me lift her up. I like putting them in while they're still alive sometimes."

Freddy's last household didn't have an incinerator. "Is that how you know what happens to the assets after they've served their purpose? This household does the cleanup?"

Aimee lifted the legs and Freddy got the upper half of the woman's squirming woman's body.

"We're the only incinerator around within eighty miles. And since we're centrally located, yeah."

Freddy was frozen in time, paralyzed with fear.

"You want that keycard to see your girlfriend?" Aimee asked. "Better get to work. It's easier before they start stinking up the place and moist blood is easier to clean before it gets hard and congealed. Take my word for it."

"I didn't know. I never knew."

"Yeah, yeah, work first. We have three bodies to burn, then you can come back and clean up the floors. Scoop up what you can now so we can burn it with her. Unless you want to rape her first. Do you rape Kayla?"

"I'm not a rapist!" Freddy directed his anger towards the job, his gloved hands picking up the removed flesh and placing it on top of the woman's body that Aimee was now strapping to the gurney. "I would never hurt Kayla!"

"That's what you keep telling me. I might just believe you."

Some of the loose skin was rolled over itself like the discarded peel of carrots, blood pooling in the centers of the spheres. "Do you people have no respect for human life?"

"No, we don't. Maybe that's why we work here. But we do follow rules and take care of our own."

Freddy wasn't sure what that meant, but he continued to pick up the tattered pieces of human skin from the floor.

+++++++++

The incineration process was not easy physically. Transferring the three bodies from the gurney to the cremation furnace was taxing.

Aimee squealed with excitement as they loaded the still alive woman on the table that slid out of the cremation furnace. With the majority of her flesh removed, she was in shock and no longer fighting, but half aware of her surroundings.

As they loaded the woman onto the sliding table, Aimee quickly rolled it back inside the machine, and slammed the door, clanging metal on metal.

The small window was just enough for Aimee to look inside and give the woman a wave of goodbye. "Do you want to see this?"

Freddy didn't, but curiosity got the better of him and he stole a glance and saw the woman found the strength to raise her arms like she was reaching for some sort of exit. An exit that she wouldn't find. The narrow passageway in which she lay would be the last thing she ever saw, surrounded by ashes of the many corpses burned before her.

"See her face? It's hard to hear, but I can tell. She's

screaming!"

"You're sick," Freddy said tersely.

"Maybe so, but I didn't lock my girlfriend in this place and doom her to death. The live ones are so much more fun. After we burn all three of them, and you hose down the rooms, we'll discuss giving you your keycard."

Aimee pressed a button and flames engulfed the viewing window.

HOSED

Freddy still didn't have a keycard, but Aimee unlocked the doors to the three personal rooms, gave him a hose (long enough to reach each of the rooms), bleach, mop, and showed him where all the drains were. "Just spray it clean. Use the bleach where it's already dried. It's self-explanatory, then we'll see about getting you your keycard."

Freddy worked with a purpose, knowing he was one step closer to seeing Kayla.

+ + + + +

Aimee made it upstairs before Dex left.

"What do we think of pretty boy?"

"Do you think that asset is his girlfriend?" Dex answered her question with a question. "And if so, what do we do about that?"

"Well, can you spare a few minutes before you leave? There's only one way to find out."

+ + + + +

Freddy had a feeling that he couldn't shake. It wasn't that he felt like he was being watched because he knew he was being watched by the cameras. It felt more like paranoia, like he didn't trust his new co-workers, worried about what they might do to him if he hadn't passed their tests for joining their household.

Slopping up and spraying away blood was a mindless task, one that allowed him too much time to think. Mostly about Kayla. Had he put her in danger by telling them her name?

It was the sound of footsteps that caught his attention.

Two sets of feet walking down the hallway behind him.

Freddy exited the room he was cleaning just in time to see Aimee and Dex, walking together. They disappeared into a door down the hall, and Freddy hoped it wasn't Kayla's room. There was no way of knowing if it was Kayla's room.

++++++

"You know the pretty boy?" Aimee asked as soon as she entered the room.

Kayla was thrown off guard. After long periods of nothing, of silence and sleep and drug-induced grogginess, the sudden entrance disturbed her.

"Who is he to you? Freddy?" Dex growled, nothing friendly in his words.

"He- he brought me here," Kayla stammered,

eyeing Dexter, hoping he wasn't the co-worker that Freddy had complained about. It took several seconds but she recognized him as one of the faces she had seen right before she took a needle in her neck.

Aimee crossed her arms and frowned. "Is he your boyfriend?"

Kayla didn't know how to answer. The truth seemed to be best. "Sort of. I think."

"Yes or no?" Dex demanded. "It's an easy question. How well do you know him?"

"I- I," Kayla bit her bottom lip and paused. "I met him online a few months ago. We had a couple of dates. He tried to feed me hair, and when I didn't eat, I woke up here."

Aimee's face seemed to soften "Did he rape you?"

"I don't think so. I hope not." Kayla hoped she didn't sound weak and defeated, but she knew that she did. "I've been drugged a couple of times."

Aimee and Dex exchanged glances and left the room.

+++++

Freddy admired the clean floors and white walls, proud of himself for accomplishing his task. If anything he could prove himself to be a valuable team player in this household, which would hopefully earn the respect of his new co-workers.

Meaning that Kayla would be safer under this roof.

The sound of hushed voices carried down the hallway.

"He's crazier than we are," Aimee said in a loud whisper.

Dex didn't bother to speak quietly. "Yeah. A total freak."

"If he rapes her I swear I'll kill him."

"Well, I'll stay a bit longer. I don't want to leave you alone with him just yet. It's time we have a household meeting."

HOUSEHOLD MEETING

The disposable latex gloves and apron were a lost cause, stained red and reeked of bleach and copper. Freddy threw those out but noticed he still had some blood on his face and shirt.

He planned to first stop at his bedroom so he could take a quick shower.

Freddy tried his best to convince himself that he didn't hear what he thought he heard Aimee and Dex discussing, that it was his mind playing tricks on him. Stress seemed to affect him in unusual ways, and since he hadn't been able to see Kayla in what felt like forever, his stress level was high.

But he was stopped before.

Dex stood at the top of the stairs waiting for him. "Kitchen now."

"Can I wash up first?"

"No."

"Is this about my keycard?"

Dex shrugged. "It's a meeting. Now. You'll get a

chance to shower after."

Aimee was at the stove, stirring something in a pot. "You hungry? I'm making soup."

The red blotches on his wrists bothered Freddy. "I really just want to wash this blood off me."

'Use the sink," Dex told him. "That'll work for now. We'll keep this short and sweet. We're reassigning you."

The blood was now the least of Freddy's concerns. "Reassigning me? How? Why? You're not my boss."

"Actually, he is," Aimee said. "And we were told that you would probably need to be retrained. If we decided to keep you around. Just like this household is updated, so are some of our techniques."

"If I go to another household, I demand to take my assets with me!"

"Calm down," Dex said. "First, they're not your assets and we were warned about your household and the workers. The bad news is Caleb didn't make the cut. You did. Are you going to make this harder on yourself than it has to be?"

The threat wasn't lost on Freddy. Caleb had been murdered in cold blood, but under the guise they were doing it out of mercy and kindness. To put Caleb out of his pain. "If I refuse?"

"You won't. Or else." Dex's stare was cold and his words were laced with a threat.

Leaving Kayla was Freddy's second worst fear. His single worst first fear was death.

Aimee stopped stirring the soup and turned to face Freddy. "Don't look so pale, lover boy. There's always a chance you'll come back here, depending on your retraining. Luckily for you, you'll be working under Dex. One of the best."

"Aimee will handle the assets while we're gone."

"This isn't the way things work. I demand to speak to someone higher on the food chain!"

"You want to see the reports from your old household? Here you go." Dex opened a drawer and pulled out a manilla folder. "It's all in there. Retraining if possible, if not, you're disposable. Like Caleb."

"But..." Freddy could only think of Kayla. "But this can't be happening. All of a sudden you're my new bosses? A couple of psychopaths? Determining what happens to my life? My job?"

"I'd watch the tone if I were you," Dex snapped.

"I think it's romantic," Aimee cooed. "He doesn't want to leave the girl. It's borderline stalkerish, too, though. I'm still undecided. Shame you have to leave so soon, but I can hold down the fort til you return."

"And oh yeah, just so you don't get any bright ideas." Dex pulled out his phone, dialed a number, and put it on speakerphone.

DR. Santos appeared on the screen.

"Santos here. Speak."

"Yeah, I'm checking in. We're going to retrain the new guy. He's not thrilled with the idea. If you don't hear from me soon, send help."

"Crystal clear. Best of luck."

The phone went silent.

"Don't get any bright ideas," Aimee warned. "This is official now. Don't do anything stupid. Think of all of this as a way to earn your way back to this household."

If Freddy could fight the both of them, grab Kayla, and run away, they'd have to hide forever. That wouldn't be any type of life for them. "Can I at least tell her bye?"

"You probably won't be gone that long, pretty boy. Don't be so dramatic."

Freddy had no choice but to do what he was told.

A NOTE FROM THE DARK MIND OF SEA CAUMMISAR

In the opening scene of Kayla discovering hair in food, I wanted the readers to wonder about Freddy. From the time he sticks a needle in her neck, we're aware that he's a 'bad' guy.

However, I really wanted to demonstrate that there are multiple degrees of 'bad' or 'evil' types of people.

For example, I write extreme horror. Violence. The kind of stuff that I hope makes people squirm or maybe even roll their eyes at the absurdity of it all. Or laugh. Because some of it can be crazy funny.

So with the first scene of torture where Freddy removes the tongue from the girl who hadn't slept in days, I went light on the details. Trying to make it clear that Freddy wasn't happy about hurting this girl.

By doing so, when I introduced Caleb and wrote his scenes to be more detailed violence, then maybe (JUST MAYBE), Freddy didn't seem to be one of the worst human monsters. Don't get me wrong, Freddy isn't a good guy, and I realize there was no way to make readers sympathetic to Freddy's character, but that was the goal.

To show the readers that Freddy wasn't the most evil character in the story.

Of course, initially, as a reader, we didn't know that yet. We didn't really know why and what was going on. We just knew that Freddy drugged Kayla, and she woke up in some sort of 'prison' (not in the traditional sense, but I hope you understand what I mean).

Then we have Caleb. Who acts upon his primal urges, even if it hurts another person. Especially if it hurts another person.

And yeah, maybe his penis being severed isn't original. But it moved the plot forward as to how Freddy knew that Caleb wouldn't be raping Kayla.

Caleb didn't last and then we had Dex and Aimee.

Dex and Aimee are more violent, and not without the reward of sexual gratification (like Caleb).

What's worse? Mindless torture and killing? Raping?

Are there different levels of bad?

It's like the fiction I write…

People seem to hate animal abuse in fiction. People seem to hate child abuse in fiction. That sort of stuff. But if it's torture against adults, then most extreme readers have no boundaries. (Most, not all)

So I guess everyone's tolerance level varies.

The title of this one. Ethically Questionable #1.

Is it evil to conduct medical experiments on people to help aid doctors?

Is that better than what Caleb did? Better than what Aimee and Dex do?

Once again, I suppose that answer will be different for everyone.

My answer. It's fiction. Fake. None of it is real. So does it matter?

Anyway, next book... What will happen? How will Freddy be retrained? Will he find his way back to Kayla? Will they get a happily ever after? Also, what other kinds of experiments can we look forward to?

One last thing, I think it's scary to think that places like this might exist. Do they exist? Probably only within my fiction, but I can't prove nor deny it to be fact.

All this and more, coming soon.

If you want to keep up with my releases, I'm on various forms of social media, etc...

If you're like me and don't spend much time on social media, here's a good old-fashioned email. sharoncheatham81@gmail.com.

I read often and love Goodreads, too. If you want to keep up with what I'm reading, I'm Sea

Caummisar on Goodreads.

    Until then, Stay Dark My Friends,
    See ya next read,
    Your Friend,
    Sea Caummisar
    Contact Info for Sea Caummisar
    Facebook (Sea Caummisar)
    Twitter (@seacaummisar)
    Goodreads (Sea Caummisar)

See ya next read

Printed in Great Britain
by Amazon